Justin McCarthy

Serapion

And other Poems

Justin McCarthy

Serapion
And other Poems

ISBN/EAN: 9783337158187

Printed in Europe, USA, Canada, Australia, Japan

Cover: Foto ©Andreas Hilbeck / pixelio.de

More available books at **www.hansebooks.com**

SERAPION

AND OTHER POEMS

BY

JUSTIN H. McCARTHY

London
CHATTO AND WINDUS, PICCADILLY
1883
All rights reserved

TO MY FATHER

I Dedicate

THIS BOOK OF VERSES.

CONTENTS.

CONTENTS.

SERAPION.

I.

An open place in Alexandria. At the left the house
of the Præfect. At the right a temple to Venus.
Two Athanasian priests come in, running.

1ST PRIEST.

I HEAR their howls behind us, and the tread
Of mad rebellion pouring like a flood
Through all the city ways.

2ND PRIEST.

           Look to ourselves!
This is the answer to the Julian cry
Against the Christians.   Round the prison walls,
Where all this moon the Bishop George has lain
With Diodorus and Dracontius,
Charged with the grave offence of serving God,
The Pagans ravin, crying out for blood;
The air is full of noises.   Holy Mother,
They seem to bear this way!

1ST PRIEST.

Where shall we fly
When all is uproar?

2ND PRIEST.

Here, behind the temple
Of the lewd goddess we may find a port,
And mark what passes. Quick! those shouts are near.

(*The two priests hide themselves behind the
Temple of Venus.*)

A crowd of men come in, bearing the bodies of GEORGE,
DRACONTIUS, *and* DIODORUS.

ONE.

Upon the altars of the exiled gods
This gift is offered.

ANOTHER.

If the ghosts would drink
Live blood, let those the Galileans slew
Come here and lap!

ANOTHER.

Let all the birds of heaven
Welcome this carrion!

ANOTHER.

To the devouring sea
Fling we these bodies, that no loving fire
May burn their foul souls from this filth of flesh,
No kindly earth consume them day by day
With gentle rotting; but reluctant waves
Scatter their bones to farthest reach of tide.
How say ye, fellows?

ANOTHER.

To the sea with them !
The Nazarenes shall make no martyrs here,
Hoarding their limbs in mounds of holy dust ;
For who would find these bones must dive and swim,
And fight the fishes.

ANOTHER.

To the sea with them,
And no more words about it !   How now, Bishop
Great George, whose fingers itched for holy gold ?
Seek, if you will, for spoil of sunken ships,
That litter the sea's kingdom.

ANOTHER.

Never more
Shall you and yours with thievish hands outstretch
To rob a Roman temple.

ANOTHER.

Diodorus
Shall drink, methinks, his deepest draught to-night :
A greener than the Marcotic wine,
A cooler than the costly chills of snow.
And thou, Dracontius, that didst handle coins
As if their jingle mocked the moving spheres,
Shall play with dead men's fingers, taking hold
Of slimy ocean weeds and coral trees,
And the gaunt ribs of storm-defeated ships.
We'll see what welcome great Poseidon gives
To Galileans.

ANOTHER.

To the sea with them !
Over this offal we do squander hate ;
There's store of Christians still.

ANOTHER.

Away with them !
(*They rush out, carrying the dead bodies. The
two Athanasian priests come out from behind
the Temple of Venus.*)

1ST PRIEST.

If this fire burns with long-enduring flame
Our feet to-day tread close to Heaven's gate.
How say you, brother—is your soul prepared
To mount its martyr's crown with Bishop George
And those unhappy comrades of the faith
Whom the fierce rabble, with a lion's wrath,
Now mauls and mumbles ?

2ND PRIEST.

I am aye prepared,
But think the time not yet.   We are too strong
For Julian's hand to cover, crush us out
After such fashion.   He that grasps at bees
Forgets their stinging.   This is but a blaze
Of sullen anger quickened into life
By sudden triumph.   Taken unawares,
These victims were ensnared by easy death ;
No mighty loss, moreover—Arians
Of the most heretic strain, reserved for hell.
These Pagans do us service, save our pains,
And so be grateful.

2ND PRIEST.

                    I see further still
How we shall find advantage in this fray,
Taking great credit that we held our hands
From hateful Arian throats, and had no part
In their dismissal to the place of pain
By fierce idolatrous fingers.

1ST PRIEST.

                    You say well ;
Let's to our people and prepare their hearts
For all this day may gender ; swords can speak
The language of these butchers back again,
And there be hands among us quick to strike,
As Peter in his pride.

            (They go out.)

SERAPION *comes in : he is clad in skins, and his long
    tangled hair floats on his shoulders ; he has a staff in
    his hand. A crowd after him.*

SERAPION.

Woe to this evil city ! woe on woe !
Where is the heavenly fire which long ago
Shrivelled the sinful Cities of the Plain
To handfuls of grey dust ? The curse of God
Lies like a cloud above ye in the sky :
Will it not break and whelm ye who have built
High places, and have worshipped images
Of gods obscene ? May plague bewilder you !

ONE.

Who is this madman ?

ANOTHER.

'Tis a Christian wizard,
Dwells in the Nitrian desert with his tribe
Of like magicians.

SERAPION.

God of Israel,
Destroy this horde of devil-worshippers !
Hear me, who come as once Elisha came,
Preaching God's wrath to an idolatrous king ;
Hear and repent before it be too late,
And fire consume ye.

*A troop of dancing-girls come out from behind the Temple
of Venus.*

ONE DANCING-GIRL.

Lo, the marvellous man !

ANOTHER.

It is a madman or a conjuror :
One that has learnt beside the banks of Nile
How to charm serpents.

ANOTHER DANCING-GIRL.

Play to us, wizard !

SERAPION.

Silence, ye children of Aholibah !
Your painted faces and your tinkling feet
Cry out to Heaven for vengeance.

A DANCING-GIRL.

What is this ?
The old man curses !

ANOTHER DANCING-GIRL.

'Tis a Nazarene.
Come, girls, join hands, and dance before the fool
Who hates our calling.

> (*They join hands, and dance about* SERAPION,
> *who strikes at them with his staff.*)

SERAPION.

Harlots, to your holes,
And pray for pardon!

A DANCING-GIRL.

Save me from the madman!

A MAN.

Too much of this.   Let's cut this Christian's throat
And stop his curses.

SERAPION.

To the house of sin
I will adventure, and with holy hands
O'erthrow the bulk of Dagon.

> (*He advances towards the Temple of Venus, and
> ascends some of the steps.*)

In the Name
Of God the Father and of Christ the Son,
I here call down the wrath of Heaven upon
Julian, the wicked and apostate King,
And all his house of devils ; and I pray
God in His justice send the purge of fire
Upon this city.

ONE.

He blasphemes the gods.

ANOTHER.

He utters spells against the Emperor's life.
Silence the villain !

ANOTHER.

Drag him from the steps.

(*The mob rush upon* SERAPION *and seize him.
Enter from back* MAXENTIUS *and a troop of
soldiers, who force their way through the crowd
and rescue* SERAPION.)

MAXENTIUS.

What spirit of tumult rages in our streets,
Startling the wholesome day with hideous noise,
And show of weapons in unwarlike hands?
Whom have we here?

A MAN.

May it please your captainship,
This is a Galilean, who but now
Railed at the gods and cursed the Emperor,
Even on the steps of holy Venus' shrine.

THE CROWD.

Death to the wizard, to the Nazarene !

MAXENTIUS.

Silence, ye brawlers !   You, sir prisoner, speak ;
Is this charge true?

SERAPION.

May flame from Heaven burn
You and your fifty !

MAXENTIUS.

'Tis a kindly wish.
But Heaven, you see, is changeless to your spells.
These Christians woo their death, but must not die.
Bear him away ; and, fellows, to your homes.

(*The soldiers clear the place, and bear away*
SERAPION.)

Enter SEXTUS *and* PORPHYRIUS.

SEXTUS.

Your father, sir, I knew exceeding well ;
He was most kind to me, a boy, in Athens,
And I may measure gratitude with duty,
Playing your father here.

PORPHYRIUS.

I thank you, sir,
If you will aid me in my dearest wish
To join the Emperor's service.

SEXTUS.

By the wings
That wag on Hermes' heels, I will dare wager
You'll make a valiant soldier.   Julian loves
The brave broad limbs of youth, and dearly loves
The tuneful Attic tongue.   He'll rate you high,
And higher for your service to the gods
That guard Athene's city.   Just a word
Within our Præfect's ear, and you shall pass
Among his people ere he send you on
To win the Emperor's heart.   So lightly leap

From Africa to Asia, from Ecdicius
To Julian's self, the Cæsar of the gods.

PORPHYRIUS.

Of the great gods whom he has throned again
On earth, sometime dishonoured by the praise
Of this Prometheus from Judæa sprung
To scale Olympus.   Where's a Heracles
Shall set the rebel free whom Julian's hand
And the great will of Jove Olympian
Have hurled from heights of Heaven?

SEXTUS.

None, I think.

> (LALAGE *is borne in on a litter to the Temple of
> Venus.*)

But here's a goddess stronger than the gods.
Jove keep you, lady !

LALAGE (*leaving her litter*).

   Master Mars, good-day ;
There is a goddess sitting in the clouds
Who likes me better.   Jove is out of date,
And gets no grace from me.

SEXTUS.

   You do him wrong,
For he was ever a most gracious god
To all fair women.   But we serve the sun ;
Since Julian made him captain of the gods,
Hot Phœbus is our fashion.

LALAGE.

Nay, I care not ;
My goddess houses here—Pandemian Venus,
Who loves her daughters well.

SEXTUS.

A most dear goddess,
And triply blessed with such a worshipper,
To teach us how she showed when first she trod
The silver sea, whose every little wave
Curled up to kiss her feet, and, kissing, turned
To a sweet savour.

LALAGE.

This is silken speech.
Have you thrown lucky with the treacherous dice ?
Or be there big wars brewing? Something sure
Out of the common level must have chanced
To teach such courtier softness to your lips,
That better love a round rebellious oath
Than praise of ladies.

SEXTUS.

By the gods, dear queen,
You do me desperate wrong.   But go your ways :
Pray to your goddess for a kindlier light
To see poor mortals in.   Farewell, harsh lady !

LALAGE.

Farewell, sweet Sextus ! I'll to Venus' feet.
(*She enters the temple.*)

PORPHYRIUS.

Who is this goddess to my fortunate eyes
Made manifest ?

SEXTUS.

          'Tis plain you are a stranger
To ask who's she, beholding Lalage.
Why, she's our queen, man, and our goddess too :
Goddess and queen of every gallant heart
That beats for love in Alexandria.
Now, by the merry gods, you stand at gaze,
Your eyes all wonder, like the fool in the fable,
Who plucked the mantle from great Perseus' shield
And saw the Gorgon.

PORPHYRIUS.

          I am all amaze !
I did not think there lived upon this earth
So fair a creature.   Like a star she went,
That shoots across the sky ere we have time
To wish it lingered, while we frame the wish
The gods at such times grant us.   Those her eyes
Dazzle me more than your Egyptian suns—
Where may we meet again ?

SEXTUS.

          Now softly, youth ;
Draw bridle lest you fall.   Is she so fair
That you who are from Athens bend your knees
In such bewildered worship of the girl ?

PORPHYRIUS.

Mock not ; for never did Praxiteles,
Nor Phidias' self, nor cunning Calamis,
Beat out of breathing bronze or hew from stone

So fair a presence ; and her colour shames
The heavenliest hues that Polygnotus e'er,
Or wise Euphranor, to a goddess gave.

SEXTUS.

The story runs that when Apelles limned
The bright Campaspe, Alexander's lass,
He loved his model : and the kindly King,
Who, if all tales be true, had scant delight
In women and their ways, gave him the girl ;
But you, who paint the praise of Lalage
In glowing speech, must scarcely look to find
An Alexander in Ecdicius.

PORPHYRIUS.

An Alexander in Ecdicius !

SEXTUS.

The words were mine, and you have caught them well.
Why, my good Grecian, you could hardly hope
That one so fair as you have pictured her
Could go about unseen and unbeloved
In amorous Alexandria, till one
Came from Peiræus to the mouth of Nile
To find her comely.   She's our Præfect's now,
Who has been many a man's.   You find her fair,
But if you look to rise in favour here,
You'd best not envy him that comes this way—
Our worthy Præfect.   Stand apart with me ;
We'll take the happiest chance of speech with him.
All hail, Ecdicius !

Enter ECDICIUS, *attended, and* MAXENTIUS.

MAXENTIUS.

        Quintus Ecdicius,
Præfect of Egypt, Cæsar's second self!
Highest and greatest——

ECDICIUS.

          What's the news to-day?
I am weary, good Maxentius; for alas!
I slept not well last night; and, by the gods!
Were I not master in the Stoic fashion,
I might complain of this. What news to-day?

MAXENTIUS.

Will great Ecdicius let the cares of state
Weigh on his wearied mind? This, then, in brief:
This morn the angry servants of the gods
Broke through the prison, where for twice twelve days
George, the Archbishop of the Arians,
With Diodorus and Dracontius,
His friends in sin, were lodged, awaiting doom:
But these, being weary of the law's delay,
With Justice' falchion in their violent hands,
Took them and slew, and to the burying sea
Delivered their three bodies.

ECDICIUS.

         By the gods!
The slaves deserved to die, but not this fashion.
This must be looked to; let no further harm
Befall the Christians of whatever kind,
Arian or Athanasian.

MAXENTIUS.

I have taken charge ;
In proof whereof the captain of the guard
Hath here outside a fellow lost to shame,
Who in the open market-place this morn
Mocked at the gods, and made the sign of Christ
Before this temple.   There were folk about
That would have slain him, but we stayed their hands
And brought him safely off.

ECDICIUS.

The unmannered rogue !
I thought they had outgrown this childish mood,
And shaken hands with fortune.

MAXENTIUS.

Sir, the man
Is stranger to the city and its ways.
He is a knave from Nitria, who comes
On some fool's errand to his pontiff here.
Shall he be shown ?

ECDICIUS.

So—have the fellow in ;
'Twill serve to stop the yawning mouth of time
Some half an hour.

MAXENTIUS.

Bring in the Nitrian !

*Enter the Captain of the guard with soldiers ; in
the midst* SERAPION.

ECDICIUS.

Is this the man ?   Fellow, stand forth a while !
You have defied your Præfect and the gods.

If this be so it is a fearful sin,
And dread the penalty.

SERAPION.

There are no gods.

ECDICIUS.

Why, this is worse and worse !   An Atheist !
I thought you worshipped Christ.

SERAPION.

There are no gods !
There is one God, and Christ His only Son,
Born of a Virgin pure and undefiled.
Your gods are devils !

ECDICIUS.

Slave, respect the gods,
Or, by the beard of Julian, you shall die !

SERAPION.

I am prepared to die ; it frights me not.
But vengeance is the Lord's ; He will repay
My blood and all the blood of all the saints
Spilt on the shrines of those lascivious fiends
Ye call the gods !

PORPHYRIUS.

Now, by the gods, you lie !
The glorious gods above us in the clouds
Smile on their servants, and the fruitful world
Rejoices in their love.   The gods are great,
And they have triumphed ; they, the beautiful gods,
Who touched the lips of Homer, and inspired
The golden line of Sophocles, and stayed

Beside the couch of dying Socrates.
Slave of a crucified slave, the gods are great,
And with a little effort overthrow
These latest Titans.

SERAPION.

Thou blaspheming fool !
God have thee in His mercy.

ECDICIUS.

Silence, there !
Sir Christian, guard your tongue.   Who is this youth ?

SEXTUS.

Noble Ecdicius, 'tis a youth from Athens ;
His sire and I were merry friends of old ;
Is hither come with hope of serving Cæsar,
Serving Ecdicius.

ECDICIUS.

Welcome, jovial Sextus !
We had not seen you.   'Tis a gallant youth,
And shall be welcome.   Who adores the gods,
Him the gods buckler.   Give me leave awhile ;
You that are bold to babble at the gods,
You come from Nitria ?

SERAPION.

In Nitria
I live alone, a hermit of the Lord.

ECDICIUS.

What brought you thence to Alexandria ?

SERAPION.

For counsel with the Bishop of our faith,

2

How we may best these desperate times defeat,
And snap the snares of Satan.

ECDICIUS.

                  Hear me, hermit :
I am a man of peace, and your vain brawls
Pleasure me nothing.   You and yours are wont
To boast you hold the keys of those great gates
That shut what is from what is yet to be.
From forth the lips of rascal fishermen
Ye gather wisdom, find the answers out
To all the doubts that all philosophers
Have sorrowed over since Deucalion's flood :
You are droll, dreary, swaggering, boastful knaves.
But you have played your play ; the time is come
That ye should leave the stage to newer mimes,
With some more marvellous scheme of heaven and hell.
For yourself, man, 'tis but a word from me,
And I upset you on a well-squared cross
To die your master's death.

SERAPION.

                  Pronounce the word—
It frights me not ; but know ye this for certain,
That if ye murder me, ye surely bring
The guilt of innocent blood upon yourselves,
And on this city and its habitants.
For of a truth the Lord has sent me here
To howl your doom unto unwilling ears.
I have no dread to die.

ECDICIUS.

                I know, my friend,
You and your fellows court a martyr's death —

All to their taste—but you'll not die to-day.
Take him and keep him in your ward awhile,
Until my pleasure and a stiller time
Pronounce the words that set him on his way.
Then, if you're wise, you'll come not back again,
But keep your desert.   No more words : away !

SERAPION.

Roman, I neither thank thee for my life
Nor fear thy menace ; as the Lord directs
I come and go, and in the Lord's good time
Shall meet my death.   There is no God but God,
And Christ His only Son.

ECDICIUS.

                        Enough of this ;
Off to your prison !
                (The soldiers take SERAPION *out.)*
To listen while a Galilean talks,
You'd think he held the secret ; closer peer,
If you have patience and a peering mind,
And find these slaves as fierce among themselves
As all are to the world that circles them.
The Galilean has not made his ways
Plain to his people, so our Christians fall
To cutting Christian throats ; while our old friends
The gods, that have contented Julius Cæsar,
Are thrust aside for new divinity,
About whose Godhead, qualities, attributes,
No two among His worshippers agree ;
Yet each would force his fancy down the throat

Of the reluctant other.   Master Æsop
Had found more matter for his hunchback wit
In half an hour of Alexandria
With these same Galileans, than he had
In all the cocks and foxes of old Greece.
I have known men and cities, like my friend
Sea-washed Ulysses ; I have lived at Rome,
Read Epicurus ; have beheld the gods
Return in triumph at great Julian's heels ;
Yet am not half so sure of anything
As these are.   Truth's the rarest, curious thing
In matters of an aye and of a no,
In matters of the right hand or the left.
So I have found it ; but we must be patient.
    I pray your pardon, I strain courtesy ;
You are most welcome : you are from Greece, from
        Athens,
The fairest city of the fairest land
That Phœbus sees.   Beneath thy glorious skies
Beauty has set her temples, and the gods
Protect it with their blessing.   Life and art
Are wedded.   'Tis the country of a dream :
Full of fair forms, fair songs, fair shapes of women :
Statues and temples too divine for earth,
And poets that would charm the lords of hell,
As shows immortal Aristophanes.
Sir, words are barren in fair Athens' praise,
And I'll be dumb ; but as I am a man,
And as I am an artist, here's my hand ;
For your Greek speech and sacred city's sake,
You may command me.

SEXTUS.

          Spoken like Ecdicius.
What did I say, my Grecian? You have found
The very king of patrons. Fortune's face
Is puckered up with pleasant smiles for him
Who takes Ecdicius' hand.

ECDICIUS.

              You flatter, friend;
But what my poverty and fair intent
May fashion for this youth, be sure of it.
Give me your name.

PORPHYRIUS.

             I am called Porphyrius,
And am the kinsman, as I bear the name,
Of that wise Platonist who long ago
Wrote that great book against the Christians
Whose pages the malignant Constantine
Gave to the flames, a shameful sacrifice
On the strange altars. For myself, I seek
To wear a weapon in the mighty wars
That shall great Julian's valour echo down
To farthest stretch of time.

SEXTUS.

             Ecdicius,
I have a fighting instinct bids me read
The preface of a soldier's chronicle
In his brave bearing, and I ask no better
Than have him for my fellow when I go
To fight the Persians.

ECDICIUS.

        What you ask is had
Even with entreaty.   We have present need
Of gallant warriors to swell our legions ;
The Emperor calls for soldiers at my hand.
You come, sir, in strange times.   The gods return
To their old temples, and the Nazarenes,
But yesterday the rulers of the earth,
To-day are brought to their rebellious knees.
Give praise to Julian !   They'll not vex us long :
A little while, and every Christian throat
Will find a Christian knife prepared to slit it,
And Christian tongues to cry a holy deed,
And pleasing to the Lord.   The Arians
Loathe Athanasius even as they loathe
Their Evil One, who, fashioned like a lion,
Ranges the world.   I'm aweary of it !
Sure if the cynic of your Grecian tub
Came with his lanthorn, he'd have work enow
To find one honest man.

SEXTUS.

        Yes, there is one ;
The purest, noblest of his kind, the best
And bravest of all men ; upon his brow
Fair honour sits, and all immortal thoughts
Have in his tongue their habitation fixed.
Hear him but speak, we think a very god
Has passed from high Olympus to this earth
For one fair hour.   Observe him as he walks,
We think we see the king of all the world,

Whose every action, every trifling deed,
Is as a pattern for all common men
To note in wonder and for envy die.
There is no secret wisdom that the earth
Within her ancient bosom garners up
But he is master of, and can unfold
With glorious glosses, adding truth to truth,
Unto the awestruck ears of poor mankind,
Who stare like pigmies at his giant bulk,
And recognise a creature far removed
From their base fancies.   If our brains in travail
Should labour to beget some paragon,
By whom all virtues, all nobility,
All valour, grandeur, perfect rectitude,
Should in one human compass be displayed,
We could not come within a tenth of him
Of whom I speak—our glorious Emperor !

ECDICIUS.

Now by my life, my Sextus, bravely said ;
You should have ended with ' Your hands, fair friends !
There ran a well-read lesson.   Nay, I knew not
That in your bosom burnt such fiery zeal
For god or mortal—in whichever rank
You choose to place our Emperor.

SEXTUS.

                              Laugh on ;
Laugh on ; you have a cynic tongue
Spares nothing.   May not a poor soldier play
His little loyal part, and crave applause ?
It is the fashion, great Ecdicius ;
There's no such thing as over-praising Cæsar.

ECDICIUS.

Sir, you say well, and will most surely prove
A wise preceptor to our Grecian here,
Whom I beseech you bring with you this eve,
If so it suits his leisure, to our house—
Indeed, I pray you.   Till that hour farewell,
For here comes one whose beauty shames the sun.

(LALAGE *comes out of the temple and stands on
the top of the steps, while* ECDICIUS *advances
towards her.*)

Hail, heavenly Lalage, that seem'st to stand
The goddess' self upon the goddess' stairs !
Once in this city Cleopatra stood
In garb of Isis, while great Antony
Went as the god Osiris by her side ;
But thou, more fair than that lost queen for whom
One third the world was wasted, choosest well,
Shining like Venus, planet of the sea,
On our glad eyes.   And as for Antony,
The great triumvir of the world might dare
To mimic godhead ; but ourselves, more meek,
If we might old Anchises' part rehearse,
Would ask no fairer fortune, Lalage.

LALAGE.

If I were Venus, as the story runs,
These steps should burgeon roses ; but you see
They stand mere marble to mere mortal tread :
My roses must be plucked by human hands
From homely bushes.   Here's a flower for thee,

Thou new-time Antony, and there's for thee,
Grim soldier Sextus.

(She flings roses from a basket carried by a child
  to ECDICIUS *and* SEXTUS. *One falls on the*
  ground, and PORPHYRIUS *seizes it.)*

ECDICIUS.

          Hail to Lalage !
Maxentius, scatter gold among the crowd,
To teach them joy for beauty and its queen.

II.

A room in the house of ECDICIUS, *with a statue of*
Venus.

ECDICIUS, SEXTUS, PORPHYRIUS.

SEXTUS.

Some wine again ! this vintage is divine.
Never believe that old Anacreon
Wantoned with better when his mellow throat
Rippled out love-songs for the boys and girls
Dear to his Bacchic soul. The muse he loved
Inspires me from yon well-filled golden jar,
Up-bubbling to the brim. Give me again ;
It is divine, and I am made divine
In drinking to the most divinest thing
Of all the earth—a health to Lalage !

ECDICIUS.

Here's with you in that toast, for Father Jove,
Who—no offence to Cæsar—was most wise
In choice of women, never surely saw
A lass more worthy to make Juno jealous,

Not even when he tumbled all of gold
Into the wondering arms of Danæ.
And, by my soul! if Jove awoke to-day,
And walking up and down our city streets,
Should chance to peer within some pillar'd place,
And see our girl with roses in her hair,
High at the top place of some festival,
Be sure the poor Olympian heart would burn
Hotter than Cæsar's highest hecatomb;
But woe to Jove in leash of Lalage!
He'd have to coin his godhead all away,
To match that night of doubled moon and stars
Which gave the world majestic Hercules.
We've raised our prices since the hero age.

SEXTUS.

Yet if all tales be true our Lalage
Owes Father Jove a very world of thanks,
Who saved her from the Galilean madness
That swallowed up her sire and dam in Rome.
A brace of players they, and she a babe.
Some Christian villain won them to his way;
But she, poor lass, was safe in other hands:
That Libius was a famous rogue to know
The woman in the child; he kept her clear
Of Christians.   She should offer thanks to Jove
That gave her grace to break the hearts of men.

ECDICIUS.

Well may you say so; has not Lymachus
Waned from his substance to a very shadow
Of what he was since first his wandering eyes,

Obedient clients in the cause of love,
Lit on the girl, and loved her to his cost.
For she consumed him as the summer heat
Burns out the sap of once so stalwart trees,
And left him barely that within his purse
To take him swift to Julian overseas,
And buy him bread to keep his bulk alive,
While begging some plethoric dignity
To feed his starved exchequer, and lure back
The gossamer love of laughing Lalage.

SEXTUS.

'Tis a rare lass, and yet, for my poor part,
I that am fortune's soldier, scantly paid,
Know many a girl behind a tavern door
Will serve my turn as well—kiss home and hard
Cling me as close.   To every man his taste,
But when I give to any she that breathes
My gold, my comfort, and my golden chances,
Call me what fool you please!

ECDICIUS.

        O wiser words
Than ever fell from philosophic lips
Of those that trod at Epicurus' heel!
How say you, sir—is Athens still so wise
As of old time?

PORPHYRIUS.

        If I might speak for Athens,
I'd say that when we find a woman fair
We note no phrases of how far to love,
But love her with the strength of all our soul;

Because we know no better way than this
To brighten with all beauty our brief life ;
And if some girl of Aphrodita's mould,
With tender hair and eyes that shame the stars,
And fair limbs fashioned for a god's desire,
Gladden our sight and set our hearts afire :
Why, I should hold him basest of the base
Who'd lay against the kisses of her lips
The Empery of Cæsar.   All things die,
And glory lasts a day, and proud names perish :
Bright youth goes out too soon, but ere it flies
Seize with warm hands the blossom flower of love,
And for one kiss of hers, one hour's embrace,
Lose the world lightly.

SEXTUS.

    O my eloquent Greek,
'Tis merry to be young !   O blessed state,
To think and talk like that !

EDICIUS.

    Pity him not ;
Wiser, perchance, than we who measure out
Our lives and loves.   The eyes of Lalage
Are bright enough to burn old Reason up,
The pressure of her arms might overthrow
The strength of Cæsar ; but my tempered soul,
Proved like fine steel in fiery pits of love,
Is not for Lady Lalage to break
With wanton fingers.   That I love her well
I prove it when I pity Father Jove,
Knowing what it cost to bring her here to-night.

PORPHYRIUS.

To-night?

SEXTUS.

      Shall we have Lalage to-night?
Now, by the breasts of Venus, this is sport
Fit for the blessed gods; but, dearest lord,
Why comes this secret like a jewel hid
In bottom of a cup?

ECDICIUS.

      Sufficient cause:
A woman's promise is a thing of air;
But lightest of all pretty lady oaths
Is Lalage's passed word.   I dared not say
Ye shall see Lalage; but now all's well:
Her litter is this moment in the street.
There was a slave to watch, and give me sign
When first he saw the torches flaring bright
Herald her coming, like attendant stars
About their mistress moon.   Even now I hear
The bustle at my gate, and leave you thus
But for a moment ere I lead her in.   *[Exit.*

SEXTUS.

By Juno's eyes, this is the rarest news.
Porphyrius, you are pale, and drink no wine.
You have not sung one song within the week.
Is Athens then so fair, so very fair,
That merely thinking of the happy place
Makes Egypt dull; or is my lord in love?

PORPHYRIUS.

May not a man seem sorry without love?

Eros, that steeps men's souls in icy streams,
And tempers them with fiery wind of sighs,
Controls me not.　Let him seek otherwhere
If he would have fools' homage.

SEXTUS.

Very like,
But hear the footfall light of Lalage ;
Let's greet her with full cups.　Look in her eyes,
And if you then can boast you're free of love,
I'll set you straightway with the demigods,
For earth's no place for you.

(*He rises and turns to the door.*)

PORPHYRIUS (*aside, looking at the statue of Venus*).

O kindliest queen,
If ever thou on most unhappy men
Have pity, now make bold my stammering lips :
Give my eyes courage and the eagle's gaze,
That I may look on her.　Ye gods, she comes !
And o'er my soul such deadly faintness falls,
As if dark death were hid behind that curtain
To bid me rise and go.

(*The curtain is thrown back, and* LALAGE *enters
with* ECDICIUS.)

SEXTUS.

Hail, Lalage !
The first of all fair things.

LALAGE.

I thank your kindness ;
I love my name the better that it tempts

So stern a man to wash his mouth with wine.
Whom have we here?

ECDICIUS.

           This is Porphyrius, lady,
A gentleman of breeding and repute,
Come fresh from Athens.

SEXTUS.

           Like Hymettus' honey,
For 'tis a most sweet youth.

LALAGE.

           I am glad to know you, sir.

SEXTUS.

Nay, you will like him better by-and-by;
Just now he has a doting fit on him,
Which bids him frown on love, and cry, Away!
He will have nothing with such foolish play.

PORPHYRIUS.

I pray your silence.

LALAGE.

           Is it even so?
Why are you found so stern with poor God Love,
Whose music moves the dullard days to mirth,
And makes us merry?

SEXTUS.

           Aye, and makes us rich.
It girths our throat with gold, and hides our limbs
With silk of Cos, as yonder fountain hides
Its gilded fishes.

LALAGE.

Stay that liberal tongue ;
Will you not let our young Athenian speak ?

PORPHYRIUS.

Lady, he mocks me sadly.   Hold me not
The foe to Love, though truly I believe
The wise man whistles Cupid down the wind ;
Or so I think.

LALAGE.

Are you a Christian, then ?

PORPHYRIUS.

The gods forbid,
Who watch o'er Cecrops' city, violet-crowned !

LALAGE.

I thought, to look so young and speak so wise,
You surely flocked with those fantastic knaves
Who grovel to the God they crucified.

(She lies on a couch beneath the Venus.)

Eedicius, you shall fan me at my feet ;
And Sextus, you shall be my cup-bearer—
A part you love to play ; give me some wine
In show of service.

SEXTUS.

By Heaven, I would not change
My part with Ganymede to cup the gods,
While I can serve a goddess like to this
On Egypt's earth !

PORPHYRIUS.

Lady, what part for me ?

SERAPION.

LALAGE.

You can look young. We'll have your golden hairs
As pleasant symbol of ' Remember life.'
'Tis better than that vile ' Remember death '
With which old Egypt soured her festivals.

PORPHYRIUS.

So I may sit and know of Paris's joy
In first beholding Helen, I'm content,
And ask no further fortune.

LALAGE.

       Bravely said !
'Tis right that youth should be content with trifles.
You will be wiser soon. No Grecian fire
Had ever withered the brave walls of Troy,
No Grecian swords been turned on Trojan throats,
And sad Cassandra lived and died a maid,
If fate had pleased content the Dardan shepherd
With how fair Helen looked.

SEXTUS.

       Now, by the limbs
Of Dian dabbling in the water-brooks,
We put our young Athenian to the blush.

LALAGE.

Well, boys were made to blush, and why not he ?
Your health, my Sextus ; Egypt, thine as well ;
And yours, my baby Grecian. Edepol,
Have you no songs, no music ? Shall we sit
And wear each other out for lack of wit,
Or staring, fall asleep ?

3

SEXTUS.

Who looks on you
Would be content to watch until world's end—
Would we not, Grecian? and for Master Momus,
You'll find him, if you drink but deep enough,
Somewhere within that wide-mouthed golden jar.

ECDICIUS.

There is outside a Lydian harp-player
That has a store of songs, most honey sweet,
The Teian drunkard's, and the Lesbian girl's,
Who gave her body to the angry sea,
Being weary of all loves; Mimnermus, too,
Who did his best to trip the feet of time
With golden strands of song, he knows by heart,
And many another.   Shall I call him in?

LALAGE.

Yes; let us have him, so he make amends
For Sextus's vinous praises and the air
Of gravity our young Athenian wears:
A pair for all the world like Vice and Virtue
In the old tale.

ECDICIUS.

You are too cruel, lady.
Without there! Phrynichus.   [PHRYNICHUS *comes in.*
Attend me, boy;
Sing at your best, for you have such an audience
As would inspire Apollo with more heart
Than every muse's praise, and make god Pan
Play with a lustier spirit than of old;
What time he fashioned Syrinx into song,

And sent his pipings through the hollow vales
.Of green Arcadia.

                PHRYNICHUS.

       What shall I sing, my lord?

                ECDICIUS.

Lady, your choice?

                LALAGE.

       I care not what it be.
He sings best singing as the nightingale,
For pleasure in his note.

                ECDICIUS.

        So, what you will.

           PHRYNICHUS (*sings*).

    What is life if love be missing
        But a sigh?
    When my lips are tired of kissing,
        Let me die.
    Youth and love and summer weather
    All must float away together
        By-and-by.

    Chill old age, with formless sorrow,
        Soon shall creep
    O'er young limbs, and ere the morrow
        Dreamless sleep
    Drowns all memories of pleasure.
    Ah, for life's unfinished measure
        Let me weep!

                LALAGE.

Gods! what a song to drive dull thoughts away!
Had it been crooned out in some place of death,

                     3—2

Or chanted in the shade of cypress trees,
Beside an open grave, or sung to ghosts,
Waiting their oozy passage over Styx,
It might have passed ; but here it chills the air,
And dreary shadows grey, impalpable,
The spirits of lost hours, float silently,
And mock our mirth.

ECDICIUS.

You are a rascal !   Go !
Have you no other songs, that you must need
Troll us a ballad with a burden of death,
To fright our festival ?

PHRYNICHUS.

Indeed, my lord,
I meant no harm.

LALAGE.

Pray you, let him be ;
He did his best, and I am scarcely gracious
To chide his song.

SEXTUS.

Let's have some jolly stave,
Some drinking snatch of wise Bacchylides,
To wash the taste of dirges from our lips,
And drown sad fancies.

ECDICIUS.

Will you hear again ?

LALAGE.

No, let him go ; the echo of his song
Is sweet, for all its sadness, and perchance
He'd mar it if he strove to make amends.

ECDICIUS.

Hence, fellow, hence !   [PHRYNICHUS *goes out.*

SEXTUS.

                Now, by the hands of Hebe,
I had as lief a croaking raven sat
And whistled in my ear, as hear such songs !
If days are passing, Venus, let them pass ;
The grape can bring the blush of brightest youth
To withered cheeks ; the fire within the blood
Defies the wintry frost ; one might as well
Be linked with yonder howling Christian fools
If all our joys were dashed with dull regret,
Or cry, forsooth, because the sun has set.
I'll meet death like a Roman, hand to hand,
With flowers about my brows and jesting speech
Upon my lips, yet wet with wine and kisses.
Let those who like with sheepskin and with scourge
Greet the eternal lord !

ECDICIUS.

                The wise man holds,
With the lame stoic of Nicopolis,
That this poor life was only made to live
Till you are weary of the game, and then
The door is always open.

LALAGE.

                What say you,
My silent Grecian ?   Do you fear to die ?

PORPHYRIUS.

Lady, I fain would live my life out well,

Yet there be things I'd die for ; think it light,
And quit the world contented.

SEXTUS.

                    Would you die
If Lalage desired it ?

PORPHYRIUS.

          With glad heart !

SEXTUS.

Now, lady, here's young wisdom brought to earth ;
The shaft of love has pierced him through and hrough,
And he will fly no more, but hop as tame
As Lesbia's sparrow.   Hail, fair conqueror !
Only a Christian could resist those eyes,
Whose beauty shames the stars.

LALAGE.

               Only a Christian'
Are they so stalwart in their own conceit
That they can laugh at love ?

SEX TUS.

                    No Christian yet
Was ever known to laugh at anything !
They are too sourly wise to show their teeth,
Except to snarl at life, and as for love,
The madness which can make them what they are
Burns, as I take it, all their manhood out,
Or gives them else such strength to hold love down
As others know not !   Folly often gives
Most marvellous force to former feebleness.

ECDICIUS

Have a care, Sextus, how thy tongue runs tilt
Against these knaves.   Our masters yesterday ;
Now, by the grace of the high gods, no more
Than enemies alike to Jove and Cæsar ;
Yet here the dogs are many, show their teeth
Against the Julian edicts, flout the gods.
There is a brawling fellow at their head,
One Athanasius, beards the Emperor.
Had I my way, I'd lay him by the heels,
And have him to some quiet prison house,
And ere the dawn decrease him by a head ;
But 'tis not safe.   I wait the Emperor's word
To end the matter.

LALAGE.

                    Are there Christians still ?
This very day, in going to the shrine,
My litter stopped before a crowded street,
And when I wondering asked, was told the people
Were murdering a Christian.   Through the crowd
I saw an old man and a hundred hands
Dealing him blows, and blood with dust commingled
Pasting his face.   It was a villainous sight,
Yet as I leaned to look they swept him off,
And, as I heard, they hanged him by and-by ;
But I went on, and saw no more of it.

SEXTUS.

Aye ; 'twas the Bishop George, who dared to jeer
At holy things.   They gave him his quietus.
Would all were served so !

ECDICIUS.

     They are droll, these fellows !
This Athanasius, whom our Emperor hates,
Has dared, and that since Julian took the throne,
To conjure women, dames of high condition,
Into the crazy Galilean fashion.
Who knows?   We may find women even yet
To join our lonely friends who live out there
Where scorching desert stares at scorching sky.

SEXTUS.

Well, if they do, good-bye to abstinence ;
'Twill be a populous desert !

ECDICIUS.

     Wrong, my friend.
Have you not heard the tale how Anthony
Hid in the shadows of the Theban hills
His lonely life, and time and time again
Was vainly tempted by fair shapes of women,
That wooed his saintly body to rebellion,
And lost their labour, for he closed his eyes
And cursed them out of doors ?   Even Lalage
Had found old Anthony too stubborn,
And lowered her flag for once.

LALAGE.

     You are a fool !
What will you wager that I win this dotard
Back to man's elder fashion ?

ECDICIUS.

Anything—
My head, my heart, or all my house's wealth,
You could not get a smile from Anthony—
No, nor a look.

LALAGE.

Now, friends, be witnesses
Ecdicius stakes his wealth against my wit
To put some warmth into an old man's blood,
And that I take the bet.

SEXTUS.

Be wiser, lady ;
Your neighbour lures you with a jesting snare ;
For lo the withered limbs of Anthony,
That rotted while he lived, now rot in death ;
He sleeps beneath the desert where he spent
His foolish life.

LALAGE.

Now, by the blessed gods,
You put me from all patience.

ECDICIUS.

Pardon, lady !
You can make wise men foolish, brave men slaves,
And rich folk beggars.   Be content with me,
And leave old Coptic Anthony alone ;
For not the closest kisses of your lips
Could breathe a quickness where the clutch of death
Had surely closed.

SEXTUS.

Yet if you needs must try,
His very fellow lives and walks the earth.

Beyond there, in the desert ; point by point,
His life is based on that of Anthony.
Like him he starves ; like him he scourges long
His shrivelled body, till the tanned flesh tears ;
Like him outwatches all the host of stars
In ceaseless incantations, and forswears
All custom of the bath, believing it
The surest sign of virtue to be foul.
It's a disciple after Anthony's heart,
So holy and so dirty.

PORPHYRIUS.

Who is the man ?

Has he a name ?

SEXTUS.

He's called Serapion,
And lies even now within Maxentius' ward ;
He is the Captain Christian, the forefront
Of all the faithful ; could you win him, lady,
Here were a victory should make you famous
Above that Queen of Nile whose yellow hair
Bound Cæsar fast, and fettered Anthony ;
Yea, drew the great Triumvir to his death,
Then sent her spirit chasing after him,
Because she failed with chill Octavius.

LALAGE.

How say you, comrade, will you make a bet
I conquer this cold Christian ?

ECDICIUS.

Lalage,
I'll wager with my Venus all in gold,

That's fashioned after great Praxiteles,
You cannot win away Serapion
From his drear penance.

LALAGE.

         I accept the dare,
And stake against whatever fairest is
Among my treasures.

ECDICIUS.

         Hearken Lalage ;
Set me your golden self against my Venus,
And I'm content.

LALAGE.

         Now by great Hercules,
You ask too much.

ECDICIUS.

         Why, then, you fear to lose !
Just now I thought you were invincible,
And lo, you fear the venture.   Be it so ;
I knew you jested.

LALAGE.

         Nay, I jested not ;
I take your wager.   Bid your golden Venus
A long farewell, great Egypt ; she is mine !

SEXTUS.

Unless the madman be composed of bronze !
For even if the years have withered him
Heartless and bodiless, no more a man
Than yonder bust of Cæsar is a statue,
Still he has eyes, and if they see aright,
Our lady wins !

ECDICIUS.

I doubt it much, my Sextus.
There is a story, which Porphyrius here
May bear in mind, how fair Athenian Phryne,
Whom great Praxiteles loved beyond his art,
Heard idle rumours floating up and down
The streets of Pallas' city to this end,
That somewhere in the shadow of the hill
That rears its temples to Ægeus' sea,
Xenocrates, the wisest of the wise,
Living apart, as fits philosophers,
Laughed at the love of woman, laughed to scorn
Her power on man.   Straightway fair Phryne goes
At dead of night to where Xenocrates
Dwelt all alone; but, as the story runs,
Laughing she went and weeping came away,
Calling the sage a statue, and no man
To be so cold.   The moral whereof is,
That when you say our Lalage must win
I doubt it much, my Sextus.

SEXTUS.

I not at all.   If Venus still have place
Upon the throned Olympus of the gods,
Who see the stunted shadows of themselves
In all men's lives, she will not suffer it
That one who wears her beauty on the earth,
The goddess' fairest child, shall ever be
By an old man made nought of, put to rout;
It cannot be! so here with certain heart
I drink to Lalage, the conqueror.

ECDICIUS.

To Lalage, that may be conqueror !

LALAGE.

You do not pledge me, Grecian !

PORPHYRIUS.

Lady, no ;

This is the vilest jesting !   Pardon me
If I must answer so unmannerly ;
'Tis that I rate you higher than yourself,
And would not see so fair a gentle stoop
To such a quarry.   This Serapion—
What is he that the treasure of your lips
Should so be squandered, that the living fire
Which lies within the hollow of your hands
Should warm a madman's limbs ! The gods themselves,
Who to Hephæstus Aphrodita bound,
Would think a mortal mixture such as this
Demands a second deluge.

SEXTUS.

Excellent !

Now, Lalage, if age with golden speech,
The minted eloquence that knows not pause
Nor stammer while a coin is in the bag,
Has never laid its withered body down
Beside white limbs or twisted yellow hair
With palsied fingers, then 'twere shame indeed
To spend one kiss upon Serapion.

LALAGE.

Jest as ye will, but I will try the chance.

Give me thy signet ring, Ecdicius,
The sight whereof bids every door fly back,
And we shall shortly see how stubborn proof
Is your caged Christian to the stings of love.
Look to your Venus.

ECDICIUS.

By the blessed gods!
This is the rarest sport I ever knew,
And should be written with a golden gleam
On never-fading marble—how the queen
Of all the lovely women of the earth
Came to a prison with the merry thought
To tempt a Christian.   I could laugh till dawn
Over the sport that overtops all deeds
E'er done or dreamed by Saturn's sweetest child.

LALAGE.

Will you have done, or must I beg our Grecian
To bring me on my way?

PORPHYRIUS.

At your word, lady.

ECDICIUS.

Pray, sir, pardon me ;
I that am host here, let me play my part.
Here is our signet, lady ; we ourselves
Will bring you to the prison in whose walls
The sordid hermit sleeps.   How say ye, friends—
Shall we along and see this play out played?

III.

The prison. SERAPION *alone. A bed.*

SERAPION.

How long, oh God, shall this my pilgrimage
Creep heavily along from sun to sun
Before the end, and these world-weary eyes
Look on the glory of God's golden house?
For this have I not fasted, suffered long,
Scourged this vile body till my sinner's blood
Blackens and stiffens the lean leathern snakes
Out of their office?   Surely now the goal
Draws nearer, and I knock at heaven's gate.
Pluck open, Peter! let mine eyes behold
The many-coloured courts of Paradise,
With all the saints and angels ranged arow,
And in the midst of that great company
Some little place where I, Serapion,
May rest in peace at last; there let me bide
Quiet, and listen to the fluttered wings
Of them that flit upon the sacred stairs,
And know God's splendour by the light upon
The paly brows of holy martyrdom.
See, I am humble, Lord; I do but beg
A little place; I am not like to those,
The rash, impatient brothers, who made bold
To sit upon Thy right hand and Thy left,
Above their fellows.   What my deeds deserve
I must not say.   Lord, at Thy will the hour

That sets me free from this foul cage of flesh,
For though I truly faint not on the field,
Nor weary of the battle, it were well
To look upon Thy servant's agony,
And say 'Well done!' and snatch me up to heaven;
For what avails this further dragging on
The chain of life? All things have I performed
Unto the full, letter and spirit both;
What is there that a child of Christ essays
But I have bettered it? Eusebius
Bears on his body eighty pounds of lead—
I take a hundred; yet I keep my tongue
From plaint or boast. What though Pacomius
For fifty nights has never closed an eye?
I add ten more, and leave him far behind;
Besides that, forty days and forty nights
I keep my Master's vigil every year.
Yea, and have kept the counsel that He gave:
Sold all I had and given to the poor,
Made ceaseless prayer, nor never wasted thought
Upon the morrow. I am ready, Lord;
Why dost Thou keep Thy labourer over time?
The harvest all is reaped, the vine is pressed;
My task is over. To the watcher sleep,
To day the night, to the tired traveller rest.
Give me my wage, for nought is left to do,
And let me look in Peter's face and hear
The great key turning in the echoing gate;
And so I enter where the hosts cry out,
'Hail to the faithful one, Serapion!'
To stare upon the new Jerusalem.

The city meted with the golden reed,
Lighter than precious jasper, crystal clear,
Twelve gates, with guardian angels every one :
Its twelve foundations with apostles' names
Graven thereon.   Is there no room for mine ?
Might I not hope some space of single pearl
Should show my name in late apostleship
Written with Anthony that's gone before,
And Paul ?   Nay, nay, I do not dream of it ;
I am no peer for Paul.

     (*A knock is heard at the door.*)
         Who knocks without ?
Thy summons, Lord ? thy summons?   Woe is me !
I am on earth again.

     VOICE WITHOUT.
        Serapion.

     SERAPION.
What voice that is not of my sentinel
Salutes me with such sweetness ?   May I dream
It is some speech of holy angelhood
Bidding me rise and go ?

     VOICE WITHOUT.
        Serapion.

     SERAPION.
I come.

    (*The door opens and lets in one clad as a Pil-
    grim, with hooded face, and holding a lamp
    which is shaded by the hand*).

     PILGRIM.
   All hail, the good Serapion !

           4

SERAPION.

What would you with the sinner of that name?
The good Serapion I sought myself
These weary years, and yet I find him not.

PILGRIM.

Great master, I have crossed the livid sands
Only to kiss these holiest hands, and learn
High patience from the purest, goodliest man
That ever waited heaven.

SERAPION.

           Brother, not thus
Should one vile man greet other ; thou and I,
Fellows alike in sinning.   Is it so
Men speak of me?

PILGRIM.

         Indeed, how else! your name
Blows with each journeying wind, and the great sea
Stays not thy fame.   The edges of the earth
That groan aloud beneath the Julian hand
Echo thee on ; and every suffering church,
Voicing thy praises, bears its bruised neck
More stiffly up.

SERAPION.

        The wind goes north and south,
Ceaselessly whirling home.   The ravening sea
Swallows the mightiest floods, and is not filled.
And of the wise man no remembrance is
More than the fool.   The glory of to-day
Slips out of memory in the time to be.

So all men's praise is barren mockery.
Mouth it no more.   Serapion is dead.

PILGRIM.

Dead?

SERAPION.

Dead to all the common moods of man.
He keeps his soul in patience.   Fare you well.

PILGRIM.

Banish me not in my sore need of thee.
Hearing thee come to Alexandria
To tempt the scourge of Cæsar.   Martyrdom
Is grimly earned, and Hell's archangels triumph :
So I have crept into this hateful place,
Bribing your watch, and daring every peril,
Only to sit a little at your feet,
Learning the perfect life that no man now
May learn in this vile town.

SERAPION.

The perfect life,
Where and what is it ?   I have lived my life,
Reaching to Heaven my own way day by day.
If you have found a better, tread it out
To the end in your own fashion ; fight the fight
Like Athanasius, in the city ways,
With heathen and with heretic Arian ;
Or choose the lonely desert—who shall say
Which is the perfect, yours or mine ? who knows ?
But, both paths leading to the self-same goal,

4—2

Yours had served me, mine served your turn as well,
To bring both up before high Heaven's gate.
But in the meantime one of us will wear
The crown of all the honours of the Church,
And strive with kings, and take the earth's applause,
No doubt. I say, in all humility ;
But I will fight the prince of the power of the air
Alone, unknown, forgotten utterly.

PILGRIM.

Dear master, I would take your hand and tread
Your own hard road with joy.

SERAPION.

             The way is steep,
The burden bitter.   Many by the way
Faint and fall off, and so are lost to light.
Canst thou outwatch the courses of the stars
With sleepless lids ?   Canst thou thy body tear
With the lean thongs, till sinews, flesh, and blood
Are one ?   Or make thy couch on angry rocks,
Beneath the baneful glances of the moon,
The savage noontide sun, the torturing sand ;
Or tread on thorns without a writhen lip,
For thinking on thy Master's coronet ?
Fast close to death, and when thou needs must feed,
Feed on foul bread, and cool thy crackling throat
With water that the thirstieth wolf would spit,
Rather than swallow ?   Art thou strongly armed
At every point against the pride of Hell,
Till all temptations that the fiend can send
To stir the hidden devils of the flesh,

In shape of naked girls with wanton eyes,
Bright hair and gestures lewd, or troops of slaves
Bent with the weight of heaven-tempting gold,
Or show of meat and wine and rare perfume,
Move you no more than dancing sunlight motes
Of summer mornings?   Canst thou do all this?
If so, the desert waits thee, where to dwell
The prisoner of the Lord ; but if not so,
Turn back to men, nor vex Serapion more.

PILGRIM.

Dear saint, I loved thee for thy holy life
This many a day, and what thyself has done,
Myself may, lagging tamely off, attempt,
To do thee honour in my love for thee.

SERAPION.

Disciples I have had, but all are gone ;
And sometimes—only sometimes, understand—
On some dark day when heaven seems farther off,
I feel a little lonely.   Agarus
Was patient, and he loved his master well ;
But he has sailed long since across the sea
To Bethlehem, the birthplace of our Lord.
And wise Hippolytus, the golden-haired,
Sleeps his last sleep within the walls of Rome,
While naught remains of all he was to me
Except his book upon the Trinity,
Treasured up yonder in my desert's hut.
Sarpedon is a bishop far away
In cedar shades of blissful Lebanon.
While Basilus—I heard the news but late—

Brave Basilus embraced a martyr's death,
By order of the abominable thing
Who now defiles the throne of Constantine,
And bends his beastly front against the saints.
The burden bears down Egypt ; and the power
Of Antichrist is mighty in the land.

PILGRIM.

Alas ! alas ! for Cæsar in his scorn
Makes mock of holiest men, and gives the earth
Back to Apollo.

SERAPION.

      'Tis an evil time,
And God's own soldiers perish helplessly.
Apollo's flames are fed ; the brides of Christ
Shamefully scourged and foully done to death :
The bishops of the Lord by murderous hands
Rended like holy Arethusan Mark,
Who, fostering once the lion cub of hell,
Feels now the clutches of the elder beast.
But neither scourging nor the stings of bees,
That worked the will of Tophet on the limbs
With honey smeared, can force the stubborn tongue
To say ' All hail, Apollo !' or ' All hail,
Great Julian, warder of the people's weal ?'
I need not fear to meet a martyr's death,
Whose daily life is daily martyrdom.

PILGRIM.

Suffer me, lord, to take the place of those
Whom fortune, or the sea, or pitiless death
Have sundered from thy side.

SERAPION.

                Your voice is soft
Beyond the speech of dead Hippolytus,
And yet you spend its music foolishly,
Praying for pains too heavy for your youth.

PILGRIM.

You wrong me, master; choose what task you will:
Pluck me the sternest of thy labours out,
And I'll perform to the very top
All in your name.

SERAPION.

              All in the name of Heaven,
To whom my deeds are due. The hardest thing
My life has known—I well remember it—
When I was young and first the holy fire
Burnt in my soul, what time I lived in Rome,
I wrought my chiefest work. There dwelt a pair
In that vile city whom I saved from Hell,
Players upon the filthy Roman stage.
I shut my eyes and see them. The strong man
And the fair woman—how her golden hair
Glances like sunlight through the Roman streets!
Ah, God! they were so merry in their sin,
As if this hateful world were only made
For them to love, and laugh and juggle in.
But I, mine eyes first falling on the twain,
And seeing them so light of heart, so deep
Each in the other's love, I straightway said,
Here is a work for thee, Serapion!

Yet, knowing it were vain to speak of Christ
And of their mortal sin to such dead ears
And hearts so stirred by lust, I did a deed
Of wonder, for I sold myself a slave ;
Yea, came a Christian to lascivious mimes,
And for a space I lived their life with them,
Waited on their revels, watched them in their loves,
Eat of the bread of shame, and counted o'er
The kisses that were seals to death and Hell ;
Even as a swimmer in a raging sea
Will strive to save a drowning man I strove ;
And at the last, through all their lewd content,
They came to see my silent Christianhood ;
At first but dimly, and with laughing eyes,
But slowly with less mocking, till at last,
With counsel, prayer, and bold remonstrances,
I won them to the fold—the woman first,
And afterwards the harder mountebank—
Yea, won them from the juggling cheat of time,
And tore them from their loves, and gave their lives
To laughterless repentance for the past.
And they are long since dead, and lie apart
In holy graves.   It was a miracle.
And after that I saw the gates of Rome
For the last time, and came across the sea
To Egypt, seeking solitude, and gained
The desert, where I measure out my days
In prayer and pain.

PILGRIM.

              Dear master and dear saint,
If I dared hope for such a miracle

As this, thy triumph over lustful blood,
I should be blessed even more than now,
Kissing your hands.

SERAPION.

Your kisses burn my blood.
What faithful fervour hidden in your lips
Kindles my veins thus?   Do not hold my hands;
Kiss them no more.   O God! what dream is this?
What thing art thou?

PILGRIM.

Thy slave, Serapion;
Thy slave beneath thy feet.

(LALAGE *clings to* SERAPION, *who tries to push
her off.*)

SERAPION.

Back, devil, back;
Back in the name of God!

LALAGE.

Ah, spurn me not,
That I, a woman, sought Serapion,
And faced all dangers with no woman's fear,
To kiss thy hands and seek the light with thee!
Dear master, turn not from my womanhood;
Pity and save.

SERAPION.

Rise, woman, and begone.

LALAGE.

Banish me not, but rather pity me,
That from the proud temptations of the world,

Have fled across these evil ways to thee.
Shall it be said Serapion flung away
A human soul to darkness, just because
It wore a woman's body?   Reach thine hand;
Forget these tresses can be snares of sin;
Forget my bosom is not hard as thine;
Forget these limbs are round, and know not yet
The chastening scourge to tame their whiteness down;
Forget that woman is a thing to love;
Think only that these arms about thee held
Cling for support to the strong pillar of God;
Think only that these lips so near to thine
Thirst after truth.

SERAPION.

O God, it may be so!
Thou hast a soul to save.   I may not dare
To fling thee down a prey to nether Hell.
But hold me not, my body seems to burn;
There is a quiver in the limbs that press
So close against mine own which troubles me;
So let me go.

LALAGE.

Ah! no, Serapion.
Here, while I hold thee, I am filled with hope.
Think not my woman's blood can trouble thine.
Rather thy frozen spirit shall have strength
To cool all human pulses in my heart,
And make me wholly saint, even as thyself,
To whom I pray.

SERAPION.

A mist is on my eyes.
'Tis true that certain holy fathers bade
Defy the spirit of lust in his own field,
And in the very bed of virginhood
Sleep sinless sleep.   And I, Serapion,
Greater than they, what have I got to fear?
Woman, thy lips hold farther from my face—
Thou needst not pray so close.   Let go my robe—
I cannot for your clinging move my feet.
Why are your eyes so bright?   Ah, God! ah, God!
Is this the hour?

(He falls in a swoon.)
LALAGE.

Sad hermit, are you mine?
Or has death snatched my triumph out of hand
And given decay its own?

SERAPION.

Where is my dream?
Are you still there?

LALAGE.

Dear master, pardon me.
If it be sin to love so great a saint;
If it be sin to kiss thy lips as men
Kiss holiest relics, master, pardon me.

SERAPION.

Methought I sank into an angry sea,
The roaring water closing o'er my head,
And yet I did not drown.   What thing art thou,
That seem'st so young and fair?

LALAGE.

But a poor girl,
To whom the hovel of the anchorite
Is dearer than the palaces of kings,
Serapion a mightier name than Cæsar,
And holy homage more than human love.
You will not spurn me?

SERAPION.

Woman, kiss me not.
Thy lips will set my very blood on fire.
Thy fingers sting.   Now if I catch thee close,
And set my teeth so in that delicate throat!
Your flesh is warm and white.   How loose thy robe!
See how it slips and leaves thy bosom bare!
Ah, now it glides away!

LALAGE.

Serapion,
Kiss harder yet.   Do as you will with me!
I'll bite your brown throat through!

SERAPION.

Down, devil, down!
Thou naked image of incarnate lust,
Flung forth of Hell to set my soul on fire,
Down, in the name of God!

(*He flings her to the ground.*)

LALAGE.

Serapion,
Why do you hurt me thus?

SERAPION.

        Be silent, fiend ;
I know thee now ; thy power is at an end.
May God forgive me ; nor kind Heaven refuse
To cleanse my soul from this foul smirch of sin !
My feet have stumbled over Satan's snare,
But I have slipped the net.

    (SEXTUS, ECDICIUS, *and* PORPHYRIUS *come in.*)

SEXTUS.

        Hands off, my friend.
This lady is not for your love or hate.
Are you tried, hermit ?

ECDICIUS.

        Gentle Lalage,
Be not afeard.   Were we not close at hand,
Who would not lower you to the lion's den,
And leave you there unguarded ?

SERAPION.

        Who are ye ?
What would ye with me in my hour of shame ?
Let me go hence, or give me up to death.
I ask no mercy.

SEXTUS.

        This is the rarest jesting.
Good hermit, if she put you to the proof,
Ye took the testing well.   Most tempered steel ;
I can conceive no better.

LALAGE.

        So I have failed—
Failed like an untaught girl in her first hour
Spent with a lover alone.   A little more,
And I had lured my goblin to the touch,
And staged him for eternal merriment.
May Venus curse him!   But I take my leave,
Hooding my unsuccessful beauty up
In this vile gown.   How strong the monster is!
He could have loved well, too.   O, wise Ecdicius,
Why, you have won, and I will pay my stake.
You speak home-truths.   Let us begone from this
I faint almost to death in this vile place.

ECDICIUS.

Then, gentlemen, away.   Porphyrius,
I have a certain message for your trust,
That must go straight to Cæsar where he camps
Beside the Asian stream.   You start to-morrow.
I pray you, lady.

     (ECDICIUS *leads* LALAGE *out.*)

PORPHYRIUS.

     What, without a word,
Without a glance!   O Zeus all merciful,
I cannot bear it ; Father, let me die!

SEXTUS.

No talk of dying.   I am sorry for you,
For in my youth I had great hurt of love,
And learned to laugh it off, and here I am,
Alive and merry, that had once wise thoughts

Of cutting through my throat for woman's sake ;
Be thou a man—think if it best becomes
To weep that you have lost a Lalage,
Or to remember there are brave ways yet
Of using life, and store of women left,
With eyes as bright, lips red as Lalage's ;
And what's more to the matter, with soft hearts
Your hands may fashion.   Get you off to Cæsar.
Do well with him ; wear out this folly of love,
And in a very little space of years
You may command like Egypt, when the girl
You covet now is old, or dead and damned ;
Pluck up, my lad, the walks of earth are wide,
And much to do before we near the end ;
The heartache soon wears off.

PORPHYRIUS.

                              I tell you, friend,
That if you held the empire of the earth
Thus in one hand, and in the other showed
One hour of her and after shameful death,
I'd have no doubt to choose.

SEXTUS.

                              Then lucky for you
I can't play fortune so.

          (PORPHYRIUS *goes out.*)

                              Now hearken, hermit :
Here are three worthy fellows, all at odds
Over a piece of tainted carrion flesh—
You, that you cannot serve her to your God,

To please him with so rare a sacrifice ;
While for her sake Ecdicius would forget
The very faith he owes to Jove and Cæsar ;
And that poor schoolboy talks of selling life,
Ere it is tasted, for some minutes spent
With one that has grown stale to half the East.
I, for my part, can thank my destiny
That the gods made one woman like another
In all essential points, and so farewell.

[*He goes out.*

SERAPION.

Give me Thy pardon, Christ, since God has willed
To tempt me as he tempted Anthony.
I thought my soul was stronger, surelier knit,
And lo, the whisper of a wanton's breath
Knappeth my pride asunder.   God is great,
And when He sees some mortal swollen big
With his own love and proud humility,
His hand, far-stretched from the immortal throne,
Touches and withers all the cloak of lies,
And bares the naked sin that Adam gave ;
O God, these pagans, in Thine own wise purpose,
Triumph, and I, Serapion, am shamed ;
My pride is shattered, at Thy feet I lie,
Waiting God's will in patience to the end.

IV.

Room in the palace of ECDICIUS, *with an altar to Apollo.*

ECDICIUS.

This is a dull world, good Maxentius,
And a most sleepy city.   Nothing stirs
Worthy a moment's wonder day by day :
Each like his fellow dwindles through the glass.
The very Galileans keep their peace,
And we for prudent reasons are content
To let them slumber safe.   What news to-day ?

MAXENTIUS.

Little, my lord.   A ship has come to port
Having on board a messenger from Cæsar,
Who will be straightway here.   The news of war
Is fortunate—'tis said the Persians fly;
Nothing beside save this, that from the Pharos,
Another ship—a galley, too, of war—
Is sighted out at sea, and in its wake
Still further sail.

ECDICIUS.

   Belike more messengers
Of Julian's fiery mind.   'Tis well, Maxentius,
I would be left alone.   Let none approach,
Unless indeed the Lady Lalage.

       [MAXENTIUS *goes out.*

I had an evil dream last night ; I dreamt
That death had taken me and Lalage,

5

And on his mighty wings had wafted us
To the chill side of Styx. Alone we stood,
Alone and shivering in the starless air ;
And at our feet the oozy water washed
With loathsome lapping ; and a silent fear
Possessed my soul, for it most strangely seemed
That we had left some well-lit festival
To pass between the gloomy gates of death
And watch that sundering stream—on the one side
Our agony, and on the other side
Thick darkness and the drear abode of Dis.
Then, as we waited, on the stream appeared
A wherry, and the form of one that rowed.
I beckoned, and he came. Ye gods, how cold
The slippery ledge where could our feet scarce cling,
As she and I—yea, I and Lalage—
Stood waiting for that fatal boat to hold
Its silent passage on that murky tide !
For round that prow the waves went noiselessly.
Then, as the boat drew nearer, she and I
Looked at each other ; and I most miserable,
I stooped and kissed that sweet small mouth of hers,
So cold with death behind, and clung to her
With a great joy to find love not forgot
In that dim kingdom of the pallid shades.
Then clinging to that last long kiss of ours,
We turned and saw the barge lay but a length
From where we stayed ; and then I saw the face
Who wafted it to shore. It was the face
Of that dark hermit, with a smile on it
Of such malignant triumph that the look

Haunts me to-day, as it would stay by me
Till I had seen the latest of my suns.
Then Lalage cried out, a fearful cry ;
Whereat, like some spell broken, all the place,
The silent stream and the grey silent rocks,
And that wild face that bent its gaze on us,
And she and I, all seemed to float away
Upon a tide of dreams ; and I awoke
With that wild cry still ringing in my ears,
And that fell visage staring into mine,
To thank the gods I had but dreamt a dream.
And when I tell it, Lalage will laugh
Her laugh, so sweet a man might die to hear :
And I shall kiss her, and it be forgot.

(LALAGE *comes in.*)

LALAGE.

So grave and full of thought ? then Lalage
Troubles the State.

ECDICIUS.

        Let all the fond world perish
Before one thought for it should be a bar
Between us twain !   But 'twas not to the State
My mind was given, but to yourself, sweet queen :
What have you there ?

LALAGE.

        Here is a thing for you
I took this moment from a fellow's hand—

A messenger of Julian's fresh from sea,
The very foam upon him, and his speech
Salt as the ocean.   He would fain refuse
The precious roll to me ; but when I frowned
And bent my forehead in Olympian wrath,
He yielded up his treasure.   Welcome me,
If not for mine own merit, for the grace
That girdles an imperial messenger.

ECDICIUS.

Angel of love, thou art more welcome here
Than Julian's herald, or than Jove himself
With all the stars about him.   Where is this letter
That knows so rare a bearer ?

LALAGE.

             Great Ecdicius,
Upon my knees I humbly offer up
The sacred characters that Cæsar's hand
Has traced on parchment, holied by his touch
Beyond the human.   Do I carry it well ?
Is it not thus that all you lesser gods,
Jove's deputies, are customed to receive
The heavenly message ?

ECDICIUS.

             Never, by thy goddess,
From such an Iris ; nor do kisses pay
The pains of Cæsar's people.

LALAGE.

              Truce ! a truce !
You do forget your letter, stay my breath,

And outrage Cæsar.   Let us both be wise.
Read you your letter ; I will stand aloof
And look wise counsel.

ECDICIUS.

So, the letter, then.

LALAGE.

Judged by your face, it is not sweet to read.

ECDICIUS.

This is a troublous time.   Here is a letter,
The latest message from the Emperor,
In which he sharply chides me that my hand
Lies on the Galileans far too light.
I'll read again the Julian words : ' I swear
By the great God Serapis, that unless
You deal severer justice to the slaves,
Yourself shall answer it.   You know my temper :
Slow to condemn, but slower to forgive ;
Look to yourself.   I hear of great contempt
Shown to the gods in Alexandria ;
And as I hear, my soul is filled with grief
And fiery anger.   Would to Jove that all
The Christian venom in one man were found,
That I might choke it there, and rid the world
Of the dark juggle !   Drive the Christians out,
Whose very breath pollutes our holy shrines !
Look to yourself, unless this thing be done.
Be firm, and fear not.'   So, ' Be firm, and fear not !'
Light words to write, and heavy words to read.
The Christian pride swells stronger day by day,

And he that tries to crush it seems a child
Lifting his little heel against a brood
Of hissing serpents.

LALAGE.

Nay, if you'll be wise
And talk great themes of State, I'll fly from you
Till you have shook this business from your mind,
And turn to lighter matters.

ECDICIUS.

Sweet, farewell !
For but a little while I think how best
To pleasure Cæsar :

(LALAGE *goes out.*)

How, indeed, I know not,
In these uneasy times.

(*A servant comes in.*)

SERVANT.

My lord, here's one
Has touched the port but now, and with the hour
Craves instant audience.

ECDICIUS.

Is it Rome, or Asia ?

SERVANT.

My lord, I think from Asia.

ECDICIUS.

Bid him enter.

SERAPION.

Enter PORPHYRIUS.

PORPHYRIUS.

All hail, Ecdicius !

ECDICIUS.
Porphyrius !
Now, by the blessed gods, what brings you here ?

PORPHYRIUS.
Great matter, for the greatest heart is cracked
The world could boast of.   Julian is dead !

ECDICIUS.
The Emperor dead ?

PORPHYRIUS.
Alas that I should say it !
His spirit has aspired to the high gods,
Who greet the friend we weep.

ECDICIUS.
Why then, indeed,
Jove's greatest image on the earth is gone.
Are you most sure ?

PORPHYRIUS.
These eyes beheld him die ;
Whereafter I made speed across the sea
To be the hateful herald of this chance.

ECDICIUS.
The manner of his death ?

PORPHYRIUS.
A soldier's death.
It was a morn of battle, and our march

Led us between a sullen line of hills,
Where the dark Persian lurked. The gods themselves,
Who teach mankind by riddles, had pronounced
The day of evil omen ; for the priests
Whispered of warnings, and man told to man
How, in the latest watches of the night,
Julian had seen his Genius, veiled and sad,
Stand by his bed ; and as he sprang from sleep
Full of that fear, he saw the God of War
Float like a fiery meteor down the sky,
Far from our Eagles. But we went our way,
Daring our fate, and fate our challenge took ;
For on a sudden from the angry rocks
The furious Persian rushed, and whelmed us up
With a great wave of war ; and in the rout
A fatal spear smote Julian, and he fell ;
At sight of which such fury filled our souls,
That never did the Romans till that day
Show how the Romans fight. We beat them back,
And had the slaughter of our foes appeased
Offended Heaven to give our Julian back,
All had been well. Alas ! it was not so.

ECDICIUS.

Died he upon the field ?

PORPHYRIUS.

                    We bore him thence
To his own tent. About his dying bed
Stood some of those who loved their master best,
To whom he whispered with his failing breath:

' Friends and companions, it is time to die.
And I have learned from my philosophy
Some lesson of the greatness of the soul
Beyond the body, and the joy we owe
To the fair hour which cuts the twain apart ;
And as a favour from the gods I take
This mortal stroke, for I have lived my life,
As I believe, with honour, and I die
Of no vile sickness, nor no furtive steel
By malice urged ; but as a brave man should,
A not inglorious death.   And weep ye not
That I, your prince, must in a little while
Be mixed with the wide heaven and all its stars.
Then bravely with his dying lips he gave
Good counsel ; prayed us, to do well for Rome,
In whom we chose to follow after him.
And so in virtue to the last he died,
And left the world to be his monument.
There is no more to tell.

ECDICIUS.

                    Farewell, great Julian !
'Tis certain that the best of us must die ;
But we may die too soon.   What name is his
Who wears the wounded purple ?

PORPHYRIUS.

                    Jovian
Is Emperor now, and Christian.

ECDICIUS.

                    Christian too !
Julian, this news will further vex thy shade

Than could the Persian arrow vex thy body.
This is grave tidings.

MAXENTIUS (*coming in*).

Look to yourself, my lord, while time remains.

ECDICIUS.

Thy message, man! Pronounce what frights thee thus
To our aspect unbidden ?

MAXENTIUS.

    Good my lord,
This is no hour for ceremonious use.
The Christians of the city everywhere
Rise up against you. Joy for Julian's death
Has stirred such fiery madness in their blood,
They dream of deep revenge on gods and men
Whom Julian loved ; so have a care, my lord.

ECDICIUS.

Command the soldiers drive the rabble home,
And there's an end.

MAXENTIUS.

    There's little help in that,
For many a soldier has a Christian heart,
But dared not say so while the Emperor lived ;
Who now, great Julian dead, proclaims his faith,
And lends as ready a hand as priest or bishop
To burn a temple or to cut a throat :
You have no service there.

PORPHYRIUS.

    Ecdicius,
Within my ship there are a score of men

Sure hearts and hands, true servants of the gods,
Will serve to sweep these Christians out of sight
With but a show of weapons.   Give me leave :
I'll to the port and bring my fellows up
While you hold parley here.   And like enough
More ships have touched from Asia ; Sextus's ship
Was close to mine all yesternight.

LALAGE (*rushing in*).

                              Alas !
What tumult fills the streets ! what dismal cries
Startle the peace of noon !   Before our gates
Wild hands are weaponed, and vile voices strain
With fearful threatenings ; and I heard but now
Your name howled out, and afterwards my name.
What does it mean ?

ECDICIUS.

                    Nay, fear not, Lalage :
'Tis but some crowd of Christians out of sorts,
Must vent their spleen with howling at our doors ;
They'll soon be gone.

LALAGE.

                    Nay, there are soldiers too,
And all around a sea of angry men
Swirl round the palace steps ; they come to kill.
Save me ! oh, save !

PORPHYRIUS.

                    There is no danger, lady.
This is but summer fury, more of noise
Than graver peril.   'Tis a feverous rage
That, whirling through sedition's tainted blood,

Puts on a mask of passion.   But ourselves,
Like wise physicians, with a show of steel
Ease the distempered body.

LALAGE.

       Who is this?
You are the Greek boy with the gracious name
Came here last year.   Oh, you are truly welcome
If you have weapons, and will scourge these slaves
Back to the kennels they have issued from!
You come from Asia, from the Emperor.
Is not all well? On both your looks I read
A sombre sorrow for I know not what;
Give me the news.

PORPHYRIUS.

I come from Asia, from the Emperor,
But not the Cæsar that my sword has served.
I may not linger longer.   I'll to the harbour.
Ecdicius will deliver up my story.
Fear thou no fear.

                        [He goes out.

LALAGE.

       From Cæsar, not from Cæsar.
What is his story?

ECDICIUS.

       It is told too soon.
Julian is dead, and in his seat there sits
A Christian Cæsar.

LALAGE.

       Then we are lost indeed!
Where can we fly? This howling herd without

Know this black news, and triumph, and we fall.
Can we not fly before their hungry hands
Tear us in pieces?

ECDICIUS.

Fly, my Lalage!
I that am Roman and commanding here!
Why would you have me fly? Take courage, sweet!
This storm will soon abate.

LALAGE.

Oh, save me! save me!
Mercy, ye gods! If I have ever spared
Fit service at your shrines, forgive me now,
And save me from this doom!

(*She falls sobbing before the statue of Apollo.*)

MAXENTIUS (*coming in*).

My lord!

ECDICIUS.

Be silent!
Fright not the woman; breathe your tidings low.
Is there great danger?

MAXENTIUS.

Imminent destruction
Hangs over all unless we quell this riot.
Porphyrius by a secret way has 'scaped
The palace, seeking through secluded streets
To gain the ships and succour; if he win,
No hostile hand preventing, to the port,
He may return in time.

ECDICIUS.

But as it is,
We tremble on the edge of Erebus—
Is it not so?

MAXENTIUS.

'Tis even so, my lord.

ECDICIUS.

I must appear, and see what virtue lies
Still in the semblance of authority
To overawe rebellion.   Lalage,
I leave you for the moment.

LALAGE.

Do not leave me!
Oh, brave Ecdicius, do not let me die!
Are you the master here, and cannot save
One wretched woman's life?

ECDICIUS.

Take courage, girl!
No danger shall address thee while I live:
Surely more needless promise never yet
Came from the lips of any breathing man!
Maxentius, take her to her room.   Myself
Must to the gates and face this multitude.

V.

An open place in Alexandria. At right, the house of the Prefect. At left, a temple of Venus.

A PRIEST OF VENUS.

The rumours of the town are dangerous ;
There is an ominous quiet, like the calm
Before the rifted heavens discharge their wrath.
What think you of it ?

ANOTHER PRIEST.

        News of Julian's death,
Coming none know from where, or borne by whom,
Ran like a conflagration through and through
The Galilean quarter, and the day
Beholds them busy as a swarm of bees
In summer-time ; from every part they muster,
Holding their slaves' heads high that yesterday
Bent low enough.

ıST PRIEST.

        But would they, think you, dare
To make a violent show ?

2ND PRIEST.

        I cannot say,
But the tale goes the new-made Emperor
Is nothing but—forgive me, gods, that say it !—
A Galilean ; at the noise whereof
These Christians, being blown up with false pride,

And our belonging with a like alarm,
Shaken from strength of custom, who shall say
What things may happen?

Enter a soldier.

SOLDIER.

To your holes, ye knaves!
Have ye no terror of the light of day
Now that the enemy, thy friend, is dead,
And Christ resumes His kingdom?

1ST PRIEST (*aside*).

Is not this
A fellow of the guard?

2ND PRIEST.

Most sure he is;
But he speaks strangely.

SOLDIER.

Do you whisper, fellows?
Are ye surprised that one who yesterday
Was of the legions of the lords of Hell,
Is fain to-day to save his soul alive?
I am a Christian. Look to yourselves, I say,
Lest hands that have been forced to feed your shrines
With incense, now should turn and offer up
The priests of Baal as sacrifice to God.
Look to yourselves!

[*He goes out.*

1ST PRIEST.

The man of war is wild!
Brother, I like him not!

2ND PRIEST.

Let us go in
And pray that pleasant Venus may avert
The threatened evil.

> (*During the last few words a beggar has entered,
> and sat at the foot of the steps leading to the
> temple.*)

BEGGAR.

Kites, crows, vultures, daws,
Pack to your nests ! it is our turn at last !
The kingdom of the beggars is at hand !
Our God has come—the God of Lazarus,
Who flung down Dives howling into hell !
'Tis well to-day to be a beggar born ;
Lepers are lucky now.

1ST PRIEST.

The man is mad !
But here come other of his kind—away !
> (*They go into the temple.*)

Enter a dancing-girl.

DANCING-GIRL.

Good-day, old master !   Here's a coin for you ;
Wish me good custom.

BEGGAR.

Whither go you, girl ?

DANCING-GIRL.

To lay these flowers at Lady Venus' feet,
And pray her keep her dancing-girl in mind,

6

And send me many lovers.   Who shall say
But the dear goddess, in return for all
My gifts of flowers and little golden toys,
May grant one day such luck as Lalage's?
She was no better on a time than I :
She worked as hard as I, and danced to clowns
For copper.   I may snare a præfect too ;
My eyes are bright as hers.

BEGGAR.

                              Be silent, girl !
Your dancing-time is over, and God's wrath
Stoops on the city.   Is not Julian dead ?
And with his death these shrines and images
Of the false gods must perish.   Dance no more,
But hide your head, and pray to angry Heaven
Forgiveness of your sins.

(*A crowd of armed Christians rush in.*)

ONE CHRISTIAN.

Glory to God, for Antichrist is dead !
The idol is thrown down, the feet of clay
That bruised our necks are broken, and the tongue
That wagged against the saints is still enough.
Jove cannot help him where he lingers now—
Hot in hell-pains.

ANOTHER CHRISTIAN.

                         Glory to God indeed
Who hath upset Apollyon, knapped in twain
The spears of sin !   How is it with thee, Julian,

Now that fire clings thee, and the undying worm
Gnaws thee for ever?

ANOTHER.

Antichrist is dead,
But not his fellows.   There are folk alive
Who should not see the setting of the sun,
If Christ indeed have triumphed.

ANOTHER.

To the pit
With all the Pagan lords!

ANOTHER.

Pluck down their gods;
Break every image; burn their temples up;
Tear out the heart of every child of sin;
Let no man live, no woman nor no child,
That hath not served the body and blood of Christ
In those dark hours wherein the faithful few
Watched for the dawn!

ANOTHER.

Brother, the dawn is come;
The sun has risen.   We who prayed for day,
Now with the daylight have our work to do.
The harvest waits for garner over-ripe.
Let every man take up his sickle and reap,
Ye labourers of the Lord!

ANOTHER.

Go, some of ye,
Call up our brothers!   Bid them gird their loins

For the great battle. Seize ye torches, swords ;
One for the shrines, the other for the throats
Of Pagans.   On the instant burn and slay !
Jehovah arms your hands !

ANOTHER.

Here is great news !
The hermits of the desert hasten here
To help the flock within the city ways
To rend the wolves that ravened yesterday.
They say Serapion comes.

ANOTHER.

Serapion comes !
The man of God is here.

(SERAPION *enters with a number of Nitrian
hermits armed with clubs.*)

SERAPION.

My brethren,
The hour is come at last.   The little cloud
That hid the fair face of the sun awhile,
Dissolves to nothing.   Julian is dead !
The cankered heart is quiet, and the lips
That gave his soul blaspheming utterance
Can lie no more ; for Antichrist is dead,
And now lies howling in the pits of hell,
Praying in vain for mercy.   God is great,
Who sent this shadow but to test our faith,
That shines more strongly through.   But now, my
      brothers,
Let not our hands lie idle from the task

The Lord hath set us, till we sweep this place
Free from its lewd idolaters, the spawn
Of that dead devil.   Drive the devil's brood
To seek their lord in Hell!

    (MAXENTIUS *appears at the palace stairs wit.*
     soldiers.)

MAXENTIUS.

              How now, ye brawlers!
Seek every man his home, and leave this place,
On pain of great displeasure.

SERAPION.

             Silence, slave!
We fear no man's displeasure, who are God's,
To do God's bidding.

CHRISTIANS.

       Death to idolaters!

MAXENTIUS.

Upon them, soldiers!   Drive the villains hence!

SERAPION.

Ye men-at-arms, the Captain of the host
Fights in our battle.   Ours is the holy legion,
And He that leads, the Saviour of the world.
Julian is dead ; that dark, rebellious angel
Who warred against high Heaven is overthrown,
And on his neck the Shepherd of the world
Plants the pierced feet of holy Calvary.
Who lifts his spear to wound the side of Christ?

MAXENTIUS.

Upon them, guards!   What, do ye falter, fellows?

A SOLDIER.

I'll lift no hand against the holy men.

ANOTHER.

I fight no battle with the cause of Christ.

ANOTHER.

I am a Christian.

OTHERS.

　　　　　　We are Christians too;
We will not fight our brothers of the faith
For the false gods of Rome.

> (*Several of the soldiers go down and mingle with
> the crowd of Christians, who clasp their hands
> and fall upon their necks.   Many kneel to
> receive the blessing of the Nitrian fathers.*)

MAXENTIUS.

Rebels and traitors!   Are no true men here?
Is this allegiance?

A SOLDIER.

　　　　　　I am no traitor, I,
But a good servant of the gods above,
And of my masters here.   What say ye, comrades?
We stand together?

OTHERS.

　　　　　　Long live Ecdicius!

MAXENTIUS.

Keep back the Christians while I warn the Præfect,
And call up other aid. (*He goes in.*)

A CHRISTIAN.

Down with the Præfect !
Down with Ecdicius !

ANOTHER.

Bring the Pagan out.
(ECDICIUS *appears with* MAXENTIUS *at the head
of the stairs.*)

ECDICIUS.

Who are ye that our quiet streets profane
With shameless clamour on a day of grief,
When all the world makes wail for Julian ?

CHRISTIANS.

Antichrist ! Antichrist ! Down with Ecdicius.

SERAPION.

Say rather that the world to-day rejoices,
Because the enemy of man and God
Has bit the dust at last, in God's good time.
And thou, Ecdicius, be prepared to stand
Before the judgment, for thy many sins ;
For all the stripes that ye have measured out
Unto the servants of the Lord of Hosts,
Shall now to thee be measured. To this end
Your heart was hardened more than Pharaoh's
To meet his doom. Ecdicius, you must die !

ECDICIUS.

You speak safe truths in saying I must die,
Who never claimed to be immortal, friend;
But that my life is yours to give or take,
I'll not believe it.   Be advised by me,
And get thee hence, or worse may come of it.

SERAPION.

Think not, thou son of Satan, with brave words
To cheat the wrath of heaven.   Your days are done;
The blood of all the holy that your hand
Has spilt, cries out for vengeance.   Nor in vain
Echoes that cry through the celestial courts.
Wherefore your time has run.   Come down and die!

ECDICIUS.

Friends all, my warning for this last time take,
And part in peace, before I sweep with steel
This wildness quiet, and once more I call
On those who serve the Eagles, to hold fast
By Jove, and by their standards.

SERAPION.

                          Hear no more!
The hand of Heaven is armed to overthrow
Lucifer's legions.   With three hundred men
The son of Joash spoiled the Midianites.
Up and upon them!

> (SERAPION *and the Christians rush to the steps
> of the palace.   The soldiers make a brief re-
> sistance, but are scattered and overpowered.*

Maxentius *is killed.* Ecdicius, *fighting
desperately, is whirled to the front, disarmed,
and seized.*)

ECDICIUS.

Ye dogs, have done !

SERAPION.

So thou art fallen, Pharaoh !
You made most merry with my hour of shame ;
Do you laugh now ?

ECDICIUS.

Aye, to the last I laugh,
For sure the gods devised you for their sport,
In scorn of nobler things.

SERAPION.

Away with him !
See him kept safely in some prison-house,
Until some fitter hour decides his doom.

(Ecdicius *is dragged out, guarded by some of
the Christian soldiers.*)

Brothers, Ecdicius holds within his house
The laughing harlot, Venus' vilest child,
The sorrow of the city, Lalage ;
Who long has worn the crown of sin, and shamed
Christ's servants.

ONE.

Give her to us, that she die !

SERAPION.

Follow and find her where she lurks within ;
But no man strike save I.

(SERAPION *and other Nitrians rush into the palace.*)

A CHRISTIAN.

Oh, glorious day !

ANOTHER.

This is the holiest hour I ever knew.

(SERAPION *appears at the head of the steps with Nitrians dragging* LALAGE.)

SERAPION.

Behold the thing,
The angel of the impious Lucifer,
That seeks to prey on souls reserved for Heaven !
It has not spread its fatal wings for flight,
But holds its human shape.

1ST HERMIT.

Spirit of Hell,
That cowerest there in shame !   By Christ His Cross,
I summon thee to quit thy present shape,
And show thyself the fiend !

2ND HERMIT.

It answers not.
Incarnate sin, I bid thee turn and flee,
Rending the lewd and lustful veil of flesh,
Back to the pits of Tophet!

3RD HERMIT.

By the blood
Of Him Who died upon the blessed tree,
I do conjure thee hence!

4TH HERMIT.

It will not go ;
But I am strong to wrestle with the fiend,
And smite it with my staff.

LALAGE.

Ah ! hurt me not.
Serapion, that art called the wise and good,
You will not let these old men murder me !
How have I done thee harm ?

SERAPION.

Thou filth, be dumb !
And ye, my brothers, seize this painted shame,
Plucked from the stench of Alexandrian stews,
To tempt the saints of God ! Lay hold of it,
And scourge its fatal spirit howling hence ;
Making this mask of carnal loveliness
Into a shape for death to shudder at.

LALAGE.

Ah, mercy, in the name of all your gods !
Forgive me ! Let me live !

SERAPION.

Take her away.
The fiend defies us. To the jaws of Hell
Beat ye his creature home.

(*As the hermits seize* LALAGE, PORPHYRIUS
*rushes in, followed by some soldiers, who drive
back the crowd a little.*)

PORPHYRIUS.

What work is here ? Let go your villainous holds !

The gods be praised that sent me here in time.
Are you hurt, lady?

> (*The hermits leave* LALAGE, *who falls on the
> ground fainting, and gather together.*)

1ST HERMIT.

Is this the Prince of Night,
Come for his demon from the caves of fire?
I have no fear.

SERAPION.

Brothers, lay hold of him!
This is some other of the spawn of sin,
By Satan sent to help this harlot here.
Shall it avail?

> (*The hermits advance on* PORPHYRIUS, *who
> draws his sword.*)

PORPHYRIUS.

Lay not a hand on me,
Or, though yourselves are old, and I am young,
I will make bold to set some blood afloat,
Now running sluggish in your villain veins.
This is my lady, and my dearly loved!
Touch her, ye kites, and, by Eternal Jove!
Your white hairs shall not save your wizard hearts
From doing strange dishonour to my sword
That serves to spit them.

3RD HERMIT.

Hear the infidel!
He calls upon the name of Lucifer!
He worships the arch-demon, the lewd god

Of Pagan beasts!   It is some imp begot
By goatish devil of a sorceress.
Pluck out his heart!

SERAPION.

Brothers, a moment's pause.
Bold youth, that stand'st here with the name of Jove
Loud in thy mouth, and brave with naked steel—
Though sword nor demon stir us—if you come,
A devil sent by devils, then this sign
Should send you howling to the gates of flame.
If you are man, what madness bids you thrust
Your feeble arm between the wrath of God
And this its victim?   Be advised, and go
And mend your life.   This woman that you see
Lies here for judgment, and must surely die.
Thou too, unless thy wisdom lead thee hence,
Repentant for thy sin.

PORPHYRIUS.

You juggling fool!
Who, howling at the gods, wouldst offer up
All loveliest things unto thy rebel God,
You shall not take my dove.   I stand alone;
But if each desert sand took human shape
More horrid than yourselves, why, here I stay.
Being better pleased to perish for her sake
Than reign in Cæsar's seat.

SERAPION.

Most pitiful,
Because most vilely snared in Satan's mesh,
Die with thy woman!

PORPHYRIUS.

A most worthy death !
Forgive me, honest sword, that I must shame thee
By letting out some misbelieving blood ;
For if we play them till the others come,
We've done our duty.   Back, ye vultures ! back !
Know that there follow, close upon my heels,
Those that shall make ye bitterly repent
Ye were so bold awhile.

SERAPION.

Hear him no more !
Seize on them both, and, by a double death,
Anger awhile Apollyon.

(*A hermit rushes in.*)

HERMIT.

We are lost !
There is a very army at our doors,
But newly come to port.

SERAPION.
Are they afar ?

HERMIT.
Woe on these lips that answer ! close at hand.
They drive our holy brothers from the streets.
Say, shall I run and rouse the city up?
We may o'erwhelm with numbers.

PORPHYRIUS.

Now the gods grant
Our friends are here in time !   Sweet lady, rise,
For all is well.

Enter SEXTUS *and soldiers.*

SEXTUS.

Hail! in the name of Rome,
What have we here?

PORPHYRIUS.

Thrice welcome, noble Sextus!
Being in time to teach these dogs a lesson,
That would have slain the loveliest thing on earth,
But for the gods.

SERAPION.

What purpose brings you here,
Ye men of Cæsar, with this armed front,
Against our quiet?

SEXTUS.

Art thou Serapion?

SERAPION.

I am the man.

SEXTUS.

Serapion, grave report
Has ever voiced you for a holy man;
Nor may I think that you maliciously,
But rather in some error of intent,
Aim at the lives of Roman citizens.
Even as I came, I heard that violent hands
Had slain Ecdicius.   Alas! the tale was true,
And I arrived too late for further use
Than to pluck back his body from the dogs
That murdered him!   This is most bloody work,
Which some have promptly paid for with their lives.
So, in the name of Rome, I here demand

You yield me up this man and woman here ;
And what complaint you have will find due ear
Before my seat in Alexandria,
Where I am mouthpiece of the Jovian mind,
That ne'er refuses justice.

SERAPION.

              This is justice,
That all who served the sinful gods should die ;
But most of all this wanton woman here.
Has she not made the holy house of God
Into a palace for the Paphian Queen ?
The shame of desolation written of
By Prophet Daniel ?

SEXTUS.

              Now, by the palm of Paul,
This is too much !   I charge ye all be still,
And hear the words of wisdom.   In your eyes
I read pale Rumour's lesson run before
To spoil my story.   Julian is dead,
And by your voices there are some be glad,
Where some draw dreary faces.   Hear me, friends !
The Apostate—enemy of God and man—
Threatens no more with sacrilegious hands
Ark, priest, and temple.   He is gone his ways—
No more of him—and in his seat there sits
Mild-minded Jovian, that most Christian king.

THE CROWD.

Jovian !   Long life to Christian Jovian !

SEXTUS.

I thank you, friends, for your fidelity ;
In proof whereof I pray you to your homes,
And make no further tumult.   Ye must know
That by the grace of God and Jovian,
Myself am Præfect here.

A CHRISTIAN.

You are no Christian !
We'll have no Præfect but a Christian here.
How say ye, brothers ?—none but Christians here !

SEXTUS.

Silence, you rascal !   By the jaws of John,
The next who lifts his voice to howl at me
Shall have rare cause for howling !   Dear my brothers,
You do me wrong with such ungentle thoughts,
That, by the mouth of Matthew, am as good
A Christian as great Jovian himself.
Let no man question this, on pain of death.

THE SOLDIERS.

Sextus the Christian, Sextus the Præfect, hail !

SERAPION.

Thou art a most ungodly man of God.
But any weapon may do holy work,
In Heaven's disposal.   By your new-found faith
I straightly charge you to deliver up
To present death this woman and this man,
Lest in your heart some lingering lust be found
After Apollyon.

7

SEXTUS.

Master Nitrian !
Within these walls 'tis I that give command,
And you that take it.   We have met of old,
And I have known you for a worthy man
And holy ; but your worth and holiness
Make you no captain here : your legions lie
Out in the desert ; better back to them,
And leave this bustle to a likelier man—
Even myself.

SERAPION.

Thou Dagon-worshipper!
Look to thyself !   And ye that hearken me,
Shall we be stayed from judgment by the speech
. Of one that bows to Baal ?   This hour is ours.
Remember ye the curse on Saul, who spared
Amalekitish cattle and its king.
Yonder is Agag, saying to himself,
' Surely the bitterness of death is past.'
Shall this be so, my brothers ?   Cry your cry—
' The sword of God and of Serapion !'

(*The mob rush threateningly forward waving their
     weapons, and shouting :* The sword of God and
     of Serapion !)

SEXTUS.

Stand back, ye brawlers ! or by Cæsar's hair
Such blood shall flow in Alexandria,
Ye'll have to swim to shelter.   Beat them back !
          (*The legionaries drive the mob back.*)

Now we can breathe ; now can our words be heard :
They are worth hearing, for they fall like pearls
From Jovian's lips, that are by me caught up
And borne with hasty speed across the sea.

ONE OF THE CROWD.

Is our new master of the Arian creed ?

ANOTHER.

Does Jovian hold with Athanasius ?

ANOTHER.

We'll have no rule of heretic Arian.
The Arian is a phase of Antichrist
Worse than the Pagan.

SEXTUS.

    Will you give me leave ?
Be sure that Jovian writes upon his heart
The heavenly words of Athanasius.
Let that suffice.   To all the Pagans here,
He in his gracious mercy deigns to grant
Perfect permission to adore their gods
In all becoming quiet, safe and sound,
Save when they deal in magic.   Ye that hear,
Store up my judgment in your memory ;
For, by the mind of Mark, I mean to keep
This city quiet.   Every man away !
On pain of grave displeasure.

A NITRIAN.

    Hark, Serapion !
Shall I with speed run through the city ways,

7--2

Rousing our warlike brothers everywhere
To fight these foemen ?

SERAPION.

              Patience, brother, patience.
In vain to strive ; the hand of Antichrist
Is armed, for reasons that we know not of,
Heavy against us. 'Tis a little while,
And these same Pagans that escape us now
Shall meet their doom : so for the hour we yield,
In hope of happier days. Severus Sextus,
You claim this woman in the name of Rome !
I claim this woman in the name of God.
Do as you will. For ye, my brothers, hence
Each to his house to serve the Lord with prayer.
      (SERAPION *goes out, followed by the Nitrians.*)

SEXTUS.

I thank you, sir, and take this lady hence.
I fear, fair Lalage, these Anchorites
Have frightened you. This old Serapion
Is tougher than you thought. Have you forgot
A certain wager?

LALAGE.

       Sextus, mock me not,
For I am sorely shamed ; but tell me, rather,
What blessed gods sent you so timely here,
Just on the word ?

SEXTUS.

       Why ! poor Porphyrius there.
Whose Greekish blood your eyes have set on fire.

Met me with wild words as I touched the port
But half an hour since—how the Christians raged
About the palace, and your life was perilled !
And scarcely tells his tale, but flies again
With some half-score of soldiers to the town.
I, knowing well the temper of these curs,
Come hasty after with my bravest men—
Who'd follow at my summons to the gates
Of golden Heaven—through the noisy streets,
At our best motion, on Porphyrius' track,
To save you both.

LALAGE.

          I thank you heartily ;
You, and my Grecian lover.

SEXTUS.

          Listen, lady !
You have two lovers.   He that holds your hand,
And Greek Porphyrius.   Brave Ecdicius dead,
I, in his place as Præfect, fain would keep
His golden bird within her golden cage.
But though I'm master here, and well might say,
' I'll wear myself the jewel I have plucked
Out of this nest of vipers, and no man
Lift up his voice against,' 'tis not my way.
Hark you, Porphyrius ! we are friends of proof ;
Here is a pretty lady seeks her mate,
With us to choose from.   You have loved her long—
Is it not so?—and as for me, my heart
Breaks for no woman.   Let her choose between.

LALAGE.

You mock me, Sextus, but you hold my hand ;
Why would you let me go?

PORPHYRIUS.

Most noble Sextus,
Believe me that I thank you from my heart,
Though not in phrases. For this lady here
I make no claim—for mine are fallen fortunes :
I should be glad to die : my days were done
When Julian perished by a nameless hand ;
And, like extinguished stars, the beautiful gods
Followed his shade into the fields of air,
And left this world to darkness. I go hence
Back to my home by the Ægean Sea,
To wear away the burden of my life
With the wise spirits of the golden past.

SEXTUS.

I pray you play the man!

PORPHYRIUS.

I am resolved ;
I have no portion here : I cannot tread
The Galilean triumph, so farewell !
I am not to be pitied that have seen
The greatest, noblest soul on earth, the last
Made in the antique fashion, and have loved
Earth's fairest woman ; and believe me, lady,
That to the latest second of my life

Your beauty shall be by me, and your eyes
Shine on me in my loneliness.   Farewell !

[*He goes out.*

SEXTUS.

Porphyrius, stay—one word !   The boy is gone.
I thought him more a soldier, for he showed
A gallant front in fight.

LALAGE.

So soft a voice,
So brave a bearing, wooed a fairer fate,
Perhaps—who knows ?

SEXTUS.

If he had been a Crœsus
You might have made a better choice than me,
Who, not for Julian, Jupiter, or thee,
Would wear such sorrow.   All the gods are good,
And any captain serves a stout man's turn ;
And if the girl I covet likes me not,
I seek some other.   But the boy will mend
With time's advances.   In the meantime, sweet,
This city's master serves you, for which grace
In these fierce times be thankful, Lalage.

IBYCUS.

Sweet sister Syrinx, has no memory hung
About your pipes of Pan, who saw you stray
With heedless feet along the river-way,
In those dear days before the gods were flung
Forth from Olympus? Are your last songs sung ?
Or will you let this piper of to-day
Make bold upon your reedy lips to play
Some of your music when the world was young—
Some music with the memory of tears
About it.   Now your voice begins to moan ;
I see a marsh land where the startled steers
Splash in the sedge ; across the red-orbed sun
The long-winged cranes fly slowly one by one ;
Down there lies slaughtered Ibycus, alone !

'Ibycus of Rhegium, having given the best part of his manhood
to the service of Polycrates, tyrant of Samos, was returning to
Corinth, where he had lived as a youth, when he was set upon
by robbers and slain.   The story goes, but I can scarcely credit
it, that as the poet was dying, he cast his eyes towards heaven,
and beholding a flock of cranes there, called upon them to
avenge him ; which indeed they did, by flying over the theatre
of Corinth on a day when the murderers were present, at sight
whereof one of these men cried out unwittingly, "Behold the
avengers of Ibycus!" and was in consequence put to death, he
and his companions.'—PAULUS HIERONYMUS. *De Poetis Infelicibus.*

A plain near Corinth.

YE mightiest gods, I thank ye that have led
My wandering footsteps to the well-beloved,

Well-wardered ways of Corinth, where she lies
. Within the shadow of the holiest hill
Wooed by the worshipping breezes.   Once again
Your temples rise before me as of old,
Filling for joy my too long alien eyes
With tears more welcome than thy fountain's wave
To weary climbers.   So I saw them last
When we were younger, I and Corinth too ;
'Twas sunrise then, and like the day my days
Were rising—had not waned to the full heat
Of manhood's summer.   Ah ! that fair June day
When I went down the pathway of the sun,
Thy walls behind me, Corinth, to the sea.
How many a year has grown from baby Spring,
With early blossoms in its golden hair,
And wide eyes wondering at the youthful world,
To lazy Winter blinking by the fire,
Since last I stared upon your sacred hill
And laughed a light good-bye !   'Twas sunrise then,
'Tis almost sunset now ; no other change.
Shall I believe this is the dying light
Of that long-distant dawn, and all the years
I wore away in Samos but a dream
As vague as that which stirred my sleep last night,
Telling me I should live a thousand years?
Close but mine eyes an instant, and I see
Myself here waiting for the last farewell,
With all my youth stretched like a widening path
Far to the golden future out of sight.
Let me behold thee.   Yet a little hour—
A little hour, and the great sun-god hurls

The latest of his fiery shafts, and leaps
All glowing downward to his deep sea halls,
Leaving this world to folded wings of night,
And the sweet service of his sister moon,
The pallid Phœbe. Ere that hour be sped
I go between the yawning brazen gates
To tread once more the old familiar streets
That watched my golden youth. O Corinth, Corinth!
There will be music in thy ways to-night,
And the red glare from lamp-lit rooms shall mix
With the wan moonlight in thy joyous streets;
For who will not make merry, who that hears
How Ibycus has wandered home again
To the sweet city? I am glad at heart
I came this way unknown, unheralded,
To steal upon my Corinth unawares,
And snare her as a lover snares his love—
Who creeps to her on tiptoe with held breath,
Laying his amorous hands about her eyes,
And with light laughter bids the startled girl
Declare who hoods her so. My name is famous
Wherever Grecian winds and Grecian waves
Fill Grecian sails, or fall on Grecian shores;
Surely most famous here, most fit for welcome;
And this night's work should overtop the mirth;
Made in the revel of that farewell night
Before I sailed for Samos over sea.
What a mad night! what merry songs we sang!
And oh, ye gods! how mightily we drank,
Shouting wild verses with the changing cups!
My head was hotter then. There was a girl—

One of the fairest I have e'er beheld—
Who fluted at that feast; and my mad blood,
Wild with the wine, and lights, and all the mirth,
Turned fire within its channels for her sake.
She stood outside in that dim portico,
Her warm flushed face beneath the golden hair
Twisted with purple roses, and the gloom
Of dark-veined ivy.   From her fingers slipped
The twin-lipped tuneful pipes.   Against a pillar,
Weary of making music, so she leaned
And panted; and I watched her bosom stir
Through the thin garment, where the leopard's skin
Had slipped away, and so I rose and passed
From the gay chamber to that pillared place
And came anigh her.   And beyond us lay
The cool dark garden, where the olive-trees
Whispered of loves.   Deep in the darkness' heart,
One nightingale its grief for Itylus
Told to the heedless stars.   A summer air,
That kissed the nodding heads of sleepy roses,
Blew on my brow, and stirred the poor dead flowers
That wreathed my brows; and silently I stared
Into my song-girl's lazy, lustrous eyes,
Thinking her worthy of that god's desire
Who guards the vineyards.   Then my flute-player,
Stirred by some frolic spirit, lightly leaned,
And struck me on the breast, and crying out,
'Follow, and find;' and shrilling laughter leaped
Into the blackness.   As a falling star
Fades into space, her body's whiteness gleamed
An instant, glancing through the mazy paths,

And vanished, and her footfalls died away.
Straightway I cried a hunter's cry, and sprang
Into the startled silence of the grove,
Stumbling between the trees with outstretched arms,
And steps that wine unsteadied, and a brain
Dizzy with riot; but they say the god
Who gave the vintage watches o'er his own.
So ran I like a satyr after nymphs,
To bring up breathless where a fountain played
Deep in the garden's core, alone, alone;
And every sound of all the sounds of night —
The sudden whirring of some startled bird,
The leaves that trembled where it passed, the fall
Of dripping water from the smooth-lipped urn—
All these were voices crying, 'Follow and find.'
But as I sank upon the grass and stared
Into the star-sown blackness of that pool,
Soft laughter thrilled me, and the gloomy wave
Mirrored her face by mine before she turned,
And laughing glided ghost-like through the trees;
But I leaped up and after swiftly ran,
And speeding, caught her as she crouched behind
Priapus' statue, and our faces met.
Strangely that long-forgotten hour floats back,
With the sharp scent of those crushed leaves, the close
Cling of her arms, the tumult of her hair,
The kisses of her lips.   Her very name
I know not, if I knew; but all next day,
What time I sailed into the open sea,
The wind seemed warm with kisses, and the air
Was heavy with the scent of shattered flowers

And close crushed leaves; and when I closed mine eyes,
Her dancing feet and tossed-back golden head
Whirled through my brain.   The creeping course of
      time
And the great life at Samos soon enough
Rubbed out the image, nor I know not now
Why such a scene as this, in such a sunset,
Calls up the spectre of that jocund hour,
And brings my youth again and the wild night
Before I sailed to Samos over sea.
The wanton boy is scarcely wiser now,
For all the shaking of Time's foolish head
And all my world of half-forgotten loves:
And if some woman's face and glorious hair
Burnt on my eyes and painted all the air
With her fair colours, I forsooth would weep
With tears as salt to leave the eyes I loved:
Wiser in this, that through my rain of tears
I should be sure that I should smile again,
Unlike the child who sees the sun to sleep,
And thinks it lost for ever.   So much gained.
What a poor beast a man is !   It is strange
That the most precious of all precious hours
Which feed the famine of devouring time
Lives in the memory with some idle toy,
Idle as this.   My chiefest hour of change,
That cuts my boy's life and my man's apart,
Lives with a flute-girl's kisses bitter-sweet.
I wonder, when my thousand years are sped,
If babbling of the flamy flesh of youth
Will seem so keen a jest?   So runs it ever,

That our most potent moments couple close
With mocking nothings, wedded, quick to dead,
Within the marriage-chambers of the mind.
Was it not so that goodliest day of days
When I stood up before the Samian Court
To battle for the lyric crown it pleased
Polycrates to offer warring bards,
And so first set my name in all men's ears,
The music of my song on all men's lips,
And built my fame its lasting monument
In all men's minds?   Between my hands the strings
Of the sweet lyre were trembling like the reeds
Within Eurotas' waters when the wind
Blows from the west, and all my soul went out
Upon the pinions of those sunset clouds
That hide the homes of gods.   The tyrant leaned,
Crushing his bearded chin into his hand,
His gaze made fast upon me ; and behold,
There came the stir of tears in his dark eyes,
That told me I had surely won my crown.
And yet, through all the sorrow of my song
And my triumphant heart, one thought prevailed
In lordship of my mind, and that same thought
How my left sandal's latchet lay unlaced,
Which thing I noticed as I rose to sing.
How my mind runs!   I shall be glad anon
When I go up into the crowded streets,
Pushing my way between the busy throngs,
To see some well-known visage lightly turn
The careless question of the town-taught stare
On one whose garb and unfamiliar face

Betrays the strayer from beyond the seas;
Then catch the sudden-lighted wonder-look
Creep in the eyes, and on my ears the fall
Of soft Corinthian speech, ' By all the gods,
But this is Ibycus!   Most welcome back!'
Then turning with that marvel on his tongue
He calls to others, ' Ibycus is here ;
Give him all hail!   Most glorious Ibycus,
The honour of our city!'   How they'll flock
Around me, as the swallows in the eaves
Greet the last swallow flying from the south,
Crowding about with noise of shrill surprise
To touch my hands, my very poet's gown,
The golden chain that great Polycrates
Gave to his singer.   So on the full tide
Of all that noisy welcome we shall float
Into some well-lit, pillared place of pride,
Where high-crowned cups that bid us quite forget
All envy of the gods and their fair drink,
Nine times more sweet than honey, shall be drained
To the sweet singer who has drifted back
To the dear home of his delightful youth,
Wherein he, henceforth weary of strange seas
And alien lands and unfamiliar speech,
Means to live out the autumn of his life,
Hold some fair house with greenest gardens girt
Find out some woman worth a poet's praise,
And throne her there and in his heart of hearts;
For I am sick of many shifting loves,
Fantastic passions veering with the wind,
Wild lights that flame and flicker like the torch

Closed in the runner's grasp that lightly goes
From hand to hand, and is blown out at last
And tossed aside unheeded.   Single love,
Like the calm beacon seen far out at sea,
Cheering with changeless purpose—single love
Is sweeter when we pass from the fierce glare
Of noontide youth, and for the first time see
That even the palace and the poet's statue
Cast a long shadow on the sunlit place.
We are no gods.   The pitiless wind of chance
Blows one by one the leaves from our life's tree,
Stripped all too soon.   Let us be wise in time :
Let even me be wise, whom fate last night
Graced with the promise of a thousand years.
A thousand years !   The colours of a dream
Are brighter than all cunning hues that men
E'er smeared a wall with ; say Apollo gives
Of this dream's thousand but poor thirty summers :
Why, I am rich indeed, for whom each hour,
To the last white-haired second, shall be full
Of joy and honour and abiding youth.
On my heart's altar I will set a flame
Steady and long-enduring ; so with love,
And restful ease, and many faithful friends,
I'll walk with patience and content at last,
Glad to be happy with the happy day,
To take all pleasures well within my arms,
Unstirred, untroubled by one vain desire.
I never yet have lived one hour of life
Out to the end ; but ever, with the cup
Raised to my lips, have sent my hopes afar

Over its edge to some diviner drink
Untasted yet, and so the cup's put down
Ere half drunk out ; but by-and-by the taste,
The rare perfume it had, come floating up,
Just as the vintage which we thirsted for
Lies laughing in its flagon to our reach.
Thus great to-morrow and glad yesterday
Have aye between them murdered poor to-day,
And robbed me of content ; nor never love
Of all the many kindly fate has given
Could drive away some glorious ghost of love,
Long dead and buried, or delight my soul
With vague assurance of immortal joy.
Those cranes float lightly through the fields of air,
Back to their reedy marshes ; every bird
As happy in his oozy osier-beds,
Where the flags float and great bulrushes sway,
As in his tyranny Polycrates,
Or I in my cloud kingdoms.   Now the sun
Shows larger in my sight before it sinks ;
The happy birds cry out their evening cry,
Whirling athwart the slowly dying disc.
I must be up and doing.   Kindly cranes,
Herald me into Corinth, seeking out
My friends of ancient days ; say Ibycus
Comes back again to rouse the startled dawn
With clamorous tongues and windy strains of song,
Blown from the flutings of uncertain lips,
And noisy laughter till the started day
Stares through the window on our flower-bound hair,
Set nodding to the triply sacred things,

Love, wine, and laughter, while the morning air
Brings to the faded blossoms of our feast
The breath of virgin roses.   All ye gods,
Behold the brightest life can promise us,
To love, to bless and bury love in wine,
And over all to laugh ; he lives who laughs.
The inextinguishable mirth of gods,
Caught up by us and echoed all along
Poor human lips, makes us a moment gods :
We laugh and seem immortal ; wherefore, Laughter,
I'll set thee up a temple over Love,
And call thee the Consoler.   Looking back
On all the hills and levels of my life,
Its plains and peaks, there is so much to smile at,
Which while I trod it out seemed grim enow,
That I henceforward with most merry heart
Shall face the world with smiles and so trick fortune,
Serving a joyous god from this hour out,
Even if I live my tale of thousand years
To its last second.

    (*He is attacked and slain.*)

     Ye cranes, avenge me !

MIMNERMUS.

There lived in sunlit Hellas long ago
A sweet-voiced singer, who has found his fame
Because he lost his love ; and so the name
Mimnermus is most dear to those who know
The song that wooed the flute-girl, and the flow
Of the sweet Grecian sorrow for the flame
Unpitied, and the universal shame
Wrought by old age on youth's triumphant show.
Time that has stopped his mouth with dust, and paled
The rose-red mouth of Nanno into clay,
Has stayed her sins and stifled his despair.
But Love has over wrinkled Time prevailed,
And so I sing Mimnermus' song to-day,
And the fair flute-girl with the sunny hair.

'Mimnermus, a poet of Smyrna, is famous by reason of his love for a flute-girl named Nanno, to whom he addressed a great quantity of verses very unsuccessfully. He is indeed a melancholy, albeit most sweet singer, full of sullen reflections on the fleetness of youth, the horrors of old age, and the delights of golden Venus.'—PAULUS HIERONYMUS : *De Poetis Infelicibus.*

A terrace overlooking Smyrna Bay.

MIMNERMUS.

I LOVE you, and I love you ; will you heed:
My songs run mad with praises of your eyes,
Whose brightness burns my soul !   Your tresses hold

My heart in golden nets : have pity, sweet,
For love has overthrown me, and I lie
A beggar at your feet.

NANNO.

     My lovesick poet,
You are the dreariest thing in all the world.
For ever swearing that my eyes are bright,
My lips are red, my tresses snares for love.
All with such wailing wonder in your voice,
As if you made a mighty voyage and found
The Fortunate Islands. Have I never known
That the high gods were pleased to make me fair,
Nor no one else until your wiseness came
Piping my charms to windy strains of song ?
Why, if I wanted lips to flatter me,
There is a mirror speaks delightful truth,
More precious than your praises ; spare your breath.
Are my eyes brighter than you find them fair ?
Or do my lips a livelier colour wear
Because you swear to kiss them were more joy
Than to command Olympus ? Are my limbs
The rounder for your verses ?

MIMNERMUS.

      Cruel girl,
Your laughter stabs my heart : I love you, sweet,
Better than life or most delightful youth,
Whose summer-tinted wings are spread for flight
Too soon, too soon ; a little while, my dear,
And thou and I are dumb.

NANNO.

               I would that hour
Had come for one I know who wastes his wit
In wearing out my patience.   Give me leave.
You come about with melancholy eyes
To tell me life is brief; I answer back,
Why should I spend one hour of it on you?
What can you give me for one golden hour—
Some sorry screed of verses?

MIMNERMUS.

              This besides,
That I can leave your name to all the world,
To make a glory of.   Fantastic Time,
That loves to shatter all delightful things,
Shall spare the fair five letters of your name,
Because a poet loved you.

NANNO.

            Craftiest bard
That ever spun out lilting line on line,
You have no wit to tell me this : my name
Sung in men's mouths long after you and I
Have suffered Time to stop our mouths with dust !
You have this power, you say ; well, be it so.
I will not prick a poet's pride with doubt,
But grant you all—full measure—even so
You will not spare your skill the more, methinks,
Because within the ledger of my loves
Your name has found no entry.   Sing away ;
Praise me or blame, and keep my name alive,

If so you please, till not a stone in Smyrna
Stands on the other ; to the end of time,
And one day after if you will—I care not.
I'll love you none the more and none the less ;
But just the same unchanging not at all,
That frights your patience : either way my gain ;
For if you pipe my praises to what tune
Of harsh or sweet you choose, by your own word
My name's immortal, and myself have lost
No hour of love upon you ; otherwise
You cease to sing, and I am plagued no more ;
Or find some other lass more lovable,
And pipe to her, and I am plagued no more.

MIMNERMUS.

Have ye no pity, gods ?   Afford me speech,
Sweet as the ring-dove voicing through the trees
Its playmate's summons ; lend my lyre such grace
As his who charmed Hell's chambers long ago,
And broke the gates of death.

NANNO.

     You conjure ill ;
Choose rather to be Jove with Danæ
Dissolving into gold : you tire me out.
Now, by Athena and Athena's owl,
Why should I love you, tell me ; and wherefore ?
Is it a mangled mumbling line or two,
Spoke with a falling whisper, full of groans
That would affright the Furies—is it this
Shall make such havoc with my skilless heart,

MIMNERMUS.

That I must fling my arms about your neck
Straightway, and kiss, and all deliver up?
Pray you, what honour or what joy to me
That such a paltry fellow sucks his lip
For passion as I pass? Vex me no more,
Or, by the gods that live in the broad heavens,
I shall find those will hound you out of doors,
And harry you from here to Pluto's house,
Where you may sing my beauty to the shades,
If them so pleases ; but to me no more.

MIMNERMUS.

Is there no way to win you to my will,
No secret science written in the stars,
Which, if I read it once, would teach my lips
The way to woo you?

NANNO.

       Here's the simplest way :
Get you a great ship with a gaudy sail,
And steer among the islands till you come
To some rich port of Egypt, where you gain,
By all the arts that cunning traders use,
Some store of golden counters ; so return.
And, while your purse such gilded words distils,
You'll see no more unkindly soul in me,
Than fierce Hermobius finds or Pherecles,
My lovers, whom you hate.

MIMNERMUS.

       A trader I?
Hang up my Lesbian lyre, and turn my hands,

That love to linger on its silver chords,
To hauling ropes instead? and tune my voice,
Not to the rise and fall of Doric strains,
But to the shouting hoarse commands at sea,
When through the creaking cordage the bluff wind
Bellows his loudest?   Oh, you surely jest!
My life was made for music and soft love;
For rose-crowned revels in some painted hall
Of nymphs and gods and graces; for long hours,
Long lazy hours beside some sacred stream,
To dream of lovely women, and to mourn
Ruin of youth.

NANNO.

'Tis your own choosing, poet;
Dream and as you will, and doze long hours away,
And waste your nights in weeping to grow old,
If such your pleasure: as for me, I care not;
But truly you will never win me thus,
Singing and sighing.   Every man his part;
If you're content with singing of your love,
While others have her, there is none to blame.
But blame me neither that I love you not,
Because you find me fair, and put your praise
In measured metre, where another tells
His tale in homely prose, but offers gifts
Worthy the Great King's consort.   You are a fool
If you seek love that can be snared by song;
There are on earth a multitude of girls
Would hear you gladly, and reward your pains
Of polished numbers with a pastoral love

Well worth the having ; wherefore come to me ?
When you drink wine you would not surely say
To him that sells the juice, 'No money, friend ;
But take a brace of verses in the praise
Of great God Dionysus, and farewell.'
You would not mock him so, yet think it strange
That I who sell the precious things of love,
Beauty and youth, should prove no greater fool
Than a poor vintner.   Had I summoned you,
Smiled when you passed or flung you down a flower
Out of my window as you went beneath,
Then might you justly blame me ; but instead,
You seek me out and say, ' Because I sing
Your praises in soft rhythms, I merit love
More than your wealthy wooers.'   Fare you well.
I am no goddess to be moved by hymns,
But one that plays the flute at rich men's feasts
For rich men's money.   Either mend your means
Or love elsewhere, and vex my life no more.

(*She goes out.*)

MIMNERMUS.

Am I a fool ? The girl is fair enough
To tempt the chiefest god.   O Queen of Love,
Why do you put such madness in the veins
Of a poor poet ? I was well enough
Making my summer music till her eyes
Shone, and I stand the saddest man on earth.

RHESUS.

'Rhesus, a king of Thrace, being promised by oracle that the town of Troy should never be taken if he fought for it, came to the leaguered city in the tenth year of the war, but was slain on the very night of his arrival by Diomede and Ulysses, as is told by Homer in his Iliads.'—MATTHEW MARVEL : *The Chronicle of Great Captains.*

THESE are the Trojan meadows, and this wind
Blows down the hollow darkness from the pines
Of Ida's mountain ; yonder moaning sound
Is the sad murmur of the Asian Sea ;
Where it receives the cool and silvery waves
Of dear Scamander ; and those points of fire
That flame against the night like fallen stars,
Those are the Grecian watch-fires.   Let them burn
For the last time to-night : a fiercer light
From the tall ships shall shine on dying eyes
Of slaughtered Greeks to-morrow ; for the hour
Has brought the hero, and the war is done.
Nor nothing save a mound of broken spears
And shattered shields, and deeply-cloven helms,
Shall leave the lightest memory to the world
How Grecian robbers crossed the writhing sea

To threat the sons of Troy with bloodied swords;
Nor any hull of all their glorious fleet
Shall breast with painted prow the purple flood,
But all burn up together.   Praise to Zeus
That has preserved me for this great emprise;
For it is written in the heavenly stars,
And muttered in the mouths of haunted caves,
And told by wrinkled wizards, and pronounced
By the oracular wind of holiest groves,
That I am called to be the doom of Greece,
The prop and stay of many-templed Troy.
For when these barbèd warders of the night
Blaze in to-morrow's heaven, the famous war
Shall be a tale for women, and the songs
Of ancient singers hymn the last great fight,
And how the Thracian Rhesus swept the Greeks
Back to the sea, and like a hunter drove
The fiery hounds of Vulcan on the ships.
Nor let great Hector blame me that my sword
Through all the wasted circle of lost years
Was busy spilling of no Grecian blood,
That I have heaped no Grecian armour up
Before my tents beside Scamander stream.
Is Troy the only leaguered town on earth?
Are Greeks the only foes? myself have fought
These weary years the angry Scythian hordes,
More harsh than hunger and more fierce than flame,
Who bayed me as in wintry northern woods
The tawny dogs their Macedonian boar
Circle with fury, whom the forest lord
Scatters with fiery rushes: never once

Have I withheld from all-delightful war
My conquering sword, nor my dear friends in Troy
Have I one hour forgotten—never yet,
While like the northern wind I cut my way
Between the Scythian spears, or stood alone
Right in the midmost of mine enemies,
Like some tall stag the hungry dogs annoy
But cannot close upon ; why, even then
My thoughts have been with Ilium, and my hand
Has deemed itself the death of Grecian men.
Yet Hector mocks me with some speech of feasts,
And rose-crowned hours of revel and light loves,
Whose couch has ever been the hollow plain,
Whose lullaby the howling Thracian wind
Coming more keen across the angry sea
Than stings of hostile arrows.   And for love—
Love I have known too little.   As I came
In triumph back from Scythia, on my way
I hunted in the angry Thracian woods ;
And there I met a maid—a huntress maid—
A very sister maid of Artemis,
Who chased the boar between the hollow hills,
And knew no fear.   Her, when I first beheld,
I loved ; and straight upon my loving spoke.
And she—for she beheld me overthrow
With one straight stroke a monarch of the woods,
And lay the dusky spoil before her feet—
She saw me more than I deserved to seem,
And chose me for her lord.   Too brief, too brief,
Our love : 'twas but a little while
I laid me down in Argathone's arms,

A hunter lover with a huntress maid,
And left the huntress maid a hero's wife.
But with my hour of rest came thoughts of Troy
Still harassed by the hungry Grecian hordes ;
And straight I led my fellows night and day
Till we could meet these Grecians face to face,
And send them howling homewards. I would fain
Deal quickly with this thing, and so return,
Leaving no Grecian on the Trojan field,
Save such as saved their souls by Styx's stream,
Waiting for Charon's coming. Argathone
Watches afar for my returning tread ;
So let me loose upon these Greeks at dawn,
And by the night I promise that no more
Sits any foe before the gates of Troy.
I am most sure of this ; the gods themselves,
Down-stooping from their awful mountain-top,
Have whispered in the ears of oracles
The certain glory of my conquering sword.
So sleep great Hector sweetest sleep this night,
Untroubled by dread dreams of darting flames
And howling women, and the rapturous yells
Of Greeks that scale the walls. The war is done !
Give me at dawn the forefront of the fight,
And ere the eve the widest Trojan waste
Shall lie as idly open to the world
As if no skimmer of the Grecian seas
Had ever strutted by Scamander stream
And cooped the sons of Priam up at home.
I hunger for the morrow morn as one
Who waits and waits outside his bridal door

Stabbed with sweet pain.   How strange it is to think
That when Jove's skyey cressets reillume,
I shall have done what I am here to do—
Shall be remembered to all time to come
For this great day !   Ye heavenly fires, good-night !
I shall sleep well, and dream of Argathone,
And paint myself that happy hour to come
When I shall say, 'Behold Achilles' shield !
Behold the helmet of great Peleus' son !
These are my spoils that smote him to the dust
And freed fair Helen and delivered Troy !'
"Twill be a blessed hour, and so good-night ;
Sleep your last sleep, Achilles.   I am come !

BRYNHILDA.

'Alors cette belle, cruelle et malheureuse femme et reine,
par ordre du roi Clotaire, fut liée à un cheval sauvage, et ainsi
horriblement mise à mort.'—AMADIS DE TOURS : *La Calandre
des Reines.*

THERE rose a sudden tumult through the night,
As down the woods that lay along the hill
A horse came plunging madly, as if strid
By some fierce fiend ; but on his steaming back
There showed no rider ; only at his heels,
Even as he fled, there fled along with him
Something that dragged and bumped upon the ground,
And dashed itself at trees and sprang from stones.
And from that fearful burden which he drew
And could not shake away, the startled steed
Leaped out into the blackness, mad with fear,
And clattered down the stony slope with hoofs
That sent the pebbles flying left and right,
And through the stream that at the foothill flowed,
Splashed with a shriek, and staggered to the field,
And stumbling, huddled in a breathless heap,
Breathed out his life.   And in the wood behind

Rose the shrill voices of a thousand birds
In noisiest clamour.　The bewildered owls
Blundered against each other in the dark ;
The jay shrilled out his questions to the thrush,
Who, in his turn, the angry nightingale
Disturbed from dreams of Philomela fair ;
The russet squirrel, from his slumber stirred,
Leaped to the topmost of the tallest trees,
And first discerned the yellow lines of dawn
Divide the darkness of the orient ;
And all the horned and dappled beasts that dwell
Within the forest hastened from their lairs
In mossy caves or by some flower-sown bank,
And glided ghostly in and out the trees,
Or creeping to the edges of the wood,
Peered down the dusky valley.　One by one
Rose up behind the swart uncleanly fowl,
Floated some ominous circles in the air,
And, croaking, wheeled along the meadow where
The horse lay shuddering, with the thing he drew
Heaped up behind him.　Round about in rows
They stood, those evil sable-plumaged birds,
With half-turned heads and bright expectant eye
Watching until the creature's agony
Should cease at last, and leave him carrion.
But while they watched, with sudden bound the dawn
Climbed up her golden stairs and scaled the sky
And a huge shoulder of Sol's scarlet disc
Thrust up beyond the meadows far away ;
And with the morn, along the woodland way,
A man came slowly.　A poor hind he was,

One from the abbey that behind the hill
Sheltered its nest of holy-hearted men.
Slowly he came, his eyes upon the ground,
Lingering along and paining his dulled brain
With wonder at the torn-up ground, the print
Of horses' hoofs, the blood about the trees,
And some few threads of twisted golden hair
Caught by the brambles. These he slowly drew
Through his hard palm, and bound in shining rings
About his fingers, by unceasing toil
Toughened to iron ; and his slow mind still
Wondered ; and as he wondered, so he came
To where the slope led down into the stream
Before the stretching meadow-land ; and there
He lifted up his eyes, and saw beyond
The ebon ranks of birds the huddled mass—
A horse and something else. Then, with a shout,
He gripped his axe, and hastened down the slope,
And sprang from stone to stone across the stream
Into the meadow ; and the dark birds rose,
Croaking their wrath into the fields of air,
While he ran up and stared upon their prey.
The horse was of a noble breed, so much
He well might guess through all the mire and foam,
And, as he hastened closer, with a neigh
It strove to rise, and gave a groan and died.
And then the churl saw how behind it lay
The body of a woman, naked, dead,
Who had been bound with twisted ropes, to trail
Behind the flying horse. 'Twas hard at first—
So torn and bruised the naked body was,

So scarred with stones and torn with thorns, so marred
With hideous blotches, shattered out of shape
In that fell journey—to be sure the thing
Was truly woman : for the golden hair,
Clotted with blood and paste of bloodied earth,
Seemed like no woman's tresses, and the breasts
Were shamed and beaten out of human grace ;
The open mouth was choked with stones and grass ;
The arms, that lay unpinioned and outstretched,
Were flayed with brambles, and one dead hand
    clutched
A screed of nettles ; and the blood ran down
The ruin of the blackened, formless trunk,
From where the pitiless cords about the feet
Ate through the tender flesh unto the bone.
Awhile the man stood silent, gazing down
On the dishonoured corpse, and made no move ;
But in his eyes the unaccustomed tears
Flowed, and about his patient heart there came
Strange pangs of pain and pity ; and he stooped
And with the knife he carried at his belt
Severed the strands that bound the dismal pair,
And bent with trembling fingers to unwind
The serpent-coils of bondage, red and stiff,
And laid the body out upon the grass,
Leaning and moaning like a wounded beast
A little ere he rose, and in his arms
Lifting the loathsome burden tenderly,
He stumbled down to where the noisy burn
Babbled and gurgled through the smoothened stones.
Then in mid flood he laid the body down,

Holding it firmly ; and the runnel ran
Wondering and bubbling through the twisted limbs,
And swift around the eddying current sped,
Staining its whirl with forest filth and blood.
Then with his hands he stayed the tide, and sluiced
With kindly cleansing water the broad thighs,
The blue-veined breasts that kingly lips had kissed,
Horribly mangled now, the broken arms
That once had tightened in their warm embrace
So many lovers ; from the gaping mouth
That had been touched so many thousand times
By such a world of wooers, this poor churl
Now washed away the mire and shameful grass,
And closed the staring eyes whose light had been
Likened to stars of heaven ; fallen stars,
Their lustre faded.   Could her lovers now
Come from their grave or from the ends of earth
To see the limbs so well-desired, so loved,
Thus lying helpless in a country brook,
The channel reddened with that queenly blood,
And only this poor slave, this woodcutter,
To be her handmaid !   On the middle stream
Her gold hair floated fan-like, freed at last
From that ensanguined paste of mire and blood.
And charitable water had restored
Something like whiteness to that tortured skin,
Whose wounds that bled no more, with livid blue,
Latticed the shapely image.   Then the churl,
Perceiving that the water's work was done,
Bore out the corpse again into the field,
To lie beneath the sun that now had climbed

A goodly height of heaven ; and by the side
He sat and watched and wept, he knew not why,
But that his mind, long deadened by harsh toil,
And his dull life no better than the beasts',
Was stirred to see so fairly made a thing
So foully treated.　Womankind to him
Was but some peasant girl about the farm,
Rough like himself, and fierce, and strong of arm,
Large handed and harsh featured, built to bear
A brood as rugged as their sire and dam.
So this white woman with the comely limbs
Made in the mould of beauty, the soft skin,
The silken hair, the curve of scornful lips,
The smooth and rounded breasts, bewildered him
With a vague marvel and a vague desire
For what he knew not : it seemed all a dream ;
But as he leaned beside the corpse and touched
With fearful hands the pale and angry face,
The poor discoloured body, the gold hairs,
There came two horsemen riding o'er the hill,
Who reined their horses on the brow and gazed
Into the meadow, saw the fallen steed,
The stretched-out body of the slaughtered queen,
And by her side the sobbing crouching slave.
Then with a shout they dashed adown the hill
And splashed across the streamlet, and rode straight
For that strange group : and as they rode, the churl,
Hearing the noise, upleaped and seized his axe,
Full of mad anger as a forest beast
Disturbed about his prey.　Then those who rode
Leaped from their seats and strode along the grass

Nigher some yards; and then one shouted out,
' How dare you meddle with the king's command ?
This is that vile Brynhilda whom Clotaire,
By grace of God the monarch of the Franks,
Has thus condemned unto a shameful death
For all her lusts and all her many sins ;
And we are bid to follow up the chase
And see the harlot in no quiet grave
Buried, but on some thrice accursed tree
Her bones shall whiten.'   So they spoke, and drew
Nearer the corpse, while the churl made no sign,
But waited while a fire within his eyes
Burned sombre ; but when one of those king's men
Raised up his arm to push the churl aside,
With a choked cry of mad unmeaning rage
He swung his axe and struck the knave to earth,
Dead, fallen on his face, and a great wound
Gaped in his throat where neck and shoulder met ;
Then with a howl the other king's fellow,
Waving his flat sword at the churl—who made
No motion towards his foe, but grimly stood
With the red hatchet poised—backed to his horse,
And leaped upon and madly whirled away,
Shrieking some words of vengeance which the wind
Scattered, and so tore clattering up the hill
And through the forest, speeding out of sight.
Then the churl went to where that other horse,
The steed of him who lay there on his face,
With trailing bridle bent and cropped the grass,
Edging a little as the man approached,
To watch his motions with unquiet eyes ;

But the churl, speaking softly with soft speech,
Came close and quickly by the bridle seized
And led him where the body of the queen
Lay, and anigh the body of the knave;
And as he came a black ungainly bird,
That from the highest trees had floated down,
Lured thither by the later scent of blood,
Rose with discordant, melancholy croak,
Back to the tree-tops and his sable peers,
A disappointed herald. Then the churl,
His arm still through the bridle, stooped and raised
The pale, insulted body of the queen
High in his arms and laid it on the horse,
Across the saddle, and secured it there
With strips of horse's gear; on the one side
The white maimed legs swung helpless, and across
The golden tresses trailed upon the ground,
And the fixed eyes stared out across the fields!
Then on the earth he wiped his bloody axe,
And with no thought of the dead man whose blood
Had smirched it, thrust the weapon in his belt,
And turning, led the unreluctant horse
Across the meadow and across the stream,
The golden tresses trailing in the flood,
Nor once looked back to notice how the birds,
The grim funereal ravens, floated down
From skyey tree-tops to the bloodied field
And settled in dark rows upon the man
Who lay there on his face, and round about
The foundered horse; but slowly went his way
Into the forest and between the trees,

By devious turnings, to his woodland eyes
Long time familiar, till at length they came
To a dim place far in the forest's heart,
Known only to himself, where never came
Men's footsteps, or the sound of hunting-horn,
Or wandering shepherd.   There he paused, and drew
The body from its place and laid it down
On the dark grass, all checkered where the sun
Played through the thickly interlacing leaves,
And o'er her limbs the shadows floated soft.
And there he tied the charger to a tree
To feed in quiet of the forest grass ;
While with his axe and his broad-bladed knife,
And with his hands, he hollowed out a grave,
And made it long and deep ; and when 'twas done
The sun had passed the zenith and begun
His gliding to the west : and all the while
The churl had worked in silence, and in peace
The horse had plucked the grasses, and the queen
Lay with the shadows floating over her ;
But now his task was ended, and the churl
Rose with a groan and o'er the body bent,
And in his eyes the tears again filled up,
While a strange crowd of unaccustomed thoughts
Thronged his numbed brain : the pity of the thing ;
The beauty of the rent, dishonoured limbs ;
The corpse that was a queen's and wore a crown
Once, like the crown the holy image wears
Within the chapel ; and had regal robes,
And many lovers, and a royal bed,

And now lay naked from a shameful death,
In that still forest, with no man save him,
The abbey serf, to find her funeral:
Such fancies, and a world of dim desires,
Coursed through his sluggard mind even as he crouched
Over the carcase that was once a queen.
But suddenly the horse, impatient, stirred
And slightly neighed; and at the sound the churl,
Startled to memory of his task undone,
Took up the queen, who for the last time lay
In any human arms, and lowered her down
In that deep hole, and with a heavy groan
Huddled the earth upon her with his hands,
And swept it with his arms into the grave
Till she was wholly hidden, heaped it up
To the grave's lips and fiercely stamped it down;
And when the work was done the sun had sunk,
Glowing a crimson circle through the trees,
Not far from setting.   Then the churl arose
Like one whom some bewildering dream has dazed,
And sprang across the horse and rode it out
Unto the farthest limits of the wood,
And there leaped off and struck it, and it sprang
Into the fields and galloped out of sight.
Then the churl hastened where the abbey lay
Grey in the valley; as he drew anigh,
From out a crowd about the postern gate
There stepped the comrade of the knave he slew
That morning, crying out, 'Behold the man!'
And straightway soldiers seized and questioned him

Where was the queen ; and when he answered not,
They tortured him, and still he made no sign,
But only groaned awhile for very pain,
And smiled to keep his secret ; and at length
They took the churl and hanged him on a tree.

THE GOLD GIRL.

(*Painting by James Whistler. Portrait of Miss Constance Gilchrist.*)

THOUGH the painter's art can show you,
    Golden lass with girlish grace,
Will an age that does not know you
    Wonder at your lovely face?
Wonder in what days Arcadian,
Such a gracious golden maiden
    Danced in such a pleasant place?

Will the world to whom we leave you,
    In your picture as you seem,
Smile and sigh, and so believe you
    Nothing but a painter's dream?
Utterly refuse to credit
That you lived in town and led it,
    That you reigned by Thames supreme?

Will the people who may view you
    In some other cycle stare,

Whispering, Is it really true you
 Had such wondrous eyes and hair?
Will they think, The painter's clever?
But we can't believe there ever
 Lived on earth a child so fair.

Shall I tell these fools who doubt you,
 How you trod with dainty feet
Many loves to dust about you?
 How our hearts were wont to beat
If by chance we saw you pass us,
Like a vision from Parnassus,
 Down some dreary London street?

You that laugh, shall we that love you
 Make these future gazers frown,
Swearing we would prize some glove you
 Once had worn, above the crown
Of our Prince or laurelled Poet,
And how proudly we would show it
 To the envious eyes of town?

They can never feel the fire you
 Cherish in your wistful eyes,
Never know how we desire you
 For the face we canonize,
For your comely close-cut tresses,
For your lips whose sweet caresses
 Well were worth a world of sighs.

Golden girl, does life content you?
 Have you played a pleasing game,

With the good the gods have sent you?
   Are you satisfied with fame?
Do you think with melancholy
That the town will feed its folly
   Sometime with some other name?

That old Time in time will claim you,
   As he claims each golden lass?
That his hands will strive to shame you,
   And the image in your glass?
For the knave has no compassion
On the form that moved our passion.
   Girls are sin—their flesh is grass.

But your picture still will match you
   With your body's graceful play,
As your lovers used to watch you
   When you danced their hearts away;
For the golden girl, beguiling
Future centuries to smiling,
   Laughs at Time and Time's decay.

And some future bard, who sees you,
   Troubled by your beauty, may
Whisper, 'Dear! I'd die to please you,
   If you danced on earth to-day!
Ah, how sweet to feel your kisses,
If you were as fair as this is;
   If to-day were yesterday!'

SONNETS.

AMOR TYRANNUS.

Now could I weep with Autumn-time betrayed
To Winter's kiss, or mourn the dateless lease
Of Death's dominion, and the chill surcease
Of youth, and beauty harshly disarrayed.
Not by the common destiny dismayed,
But grieving to behold my wisdom cease,
Since Love has rudely shattered ancient peace,
And bears at me with all his arms displayed.
Can I pluck patience from the stars, to teach
My sick soul comfort, bidding 'Be of cheer,'
That am like one who strives in vain to steer
His storm-shook vessel from some angry reach
Of dangerous rocks, where breaking terribly
Thunders the hoarse rebellion of the sea?

AUREA PUELLA.

1 CANNOT praise you : I have tried to chain
Soft rhyme with rhyme, and dainty phrase with phrase,
Into the tuneful garland of your praise ;
Which done, I straight destroy to shape again,
Doing, undoing with a world of pain ;
Twisting my verse in all fantastic ways.
But though I laboured for a year of days,
Even at the end my toil were spent in vain.
You are too fair for any praise of mine.
I will be dumb, and burn up all my rhymes.
What need to tell you you are half divine,
Who have been told so many thousand times
In sweeter fashion ?   Think of me as one
Dazzled from gazing upon Beauty's sun.

JUVENTUS MUNDI.

LET no regretful memory degrade
This gracious day from Saturn's age of gold ;
Let us believe we never shall grow old,
Nor never more this summer splendour fade ;
Let us believe no living man or maid
Shall ever lie their length beneath the mould ;
That love shall never, like a dream half-told,
Float from the merry sunlight into shade.
To-day let life be as those Tuscan tales
Of lovers hidden from the world away
In gardens where the quick-winged nightingales
Haunt the dark hollows and soft fountains play ;
Where youth is young, where passion never pales
Its scarlet lips to weep for yesterday.

IN AVALLON.

HERE, where my lazy limbs are stretched to press
The grass beneath the elm-tree's kindly shade,
I lie and watch the mellow sunlight braid
Fantastic shadows : through my drowsiness
Tricks of strange thought and fancies framed at guess
Juggle my spirit ; surely I have strayed
From the great town to some enchanted glade,
Where fair Armida holds me in duress,
Or I am prisoned in the pleasant land
Of Avallon, like Ogier, long ago,
And am content to stay : alas, the sand
Holds longer impress of the feet that go
'Twixt tide and tide, than such a summer show
May hold me captive with its fairy wand.

A GARLAND.

For you, how many a posy have I tied
Of blood-red poppies that must fade too soon,
Pale lilies with the magic of the moon
In their white petals, the imperial pride
Of starred narcissus, violets purple-eyed,
Sad hyacinthus with its written rune,
All-coloured roses the delight of June,
Anemones with blood of Adon dyed ;
For all these flowers the self-same tale repeat,
'Learn to be wise, and let no flower of spring
Go by unheeded for its odour sweet ;
For soon chill age and conquering time defeat
Love, youth, and beauty, even as they fling
A ruin of marred blossoms at your feet.'

THE BURDEN OF LOVE.

WHEN you are cruel, then the wholesome day
Sickens, and inextinguishable pain
Consumes my youth ; all beauty bears a stain ;
Unloved and tuneless runs the world away,
While its fair roses canker and decay
Before the winter of your chill disdain ;
The stars go out, the sun forgets his reign,
And sorrow rules with undisputed sway.
Then do I long for bitter words to curse
Her at whose frown all happiness has fled ;
But when rebellious fancy would rehearse
Some imprecation on your golden head,
Spite of myself the foolish faithful verse
Runs into praise and leaves the ill unsaid.

THE BELOVED.

You know not of my love, and need not know ;
Why should you heed, if once again the snare
Of those clear eyes and crown of comely hair
Have brought another victim to lie low
Before your conquering feet, that well might go
Treading on lovers' bodies everywhere?
The thing is common, and you need not care
Who have grown sick of loving long ago.
But for my part, it pleases me to lie
So in Love's chains, and dream glad hours away,
To sing your fair all other fair above.
Perchance I may prove wiser by-and-by,
And weep for this my folly ; but to-day
It pleases me to love you, and I love.

VANITY OF VANITIES.

THOUGH in my verse I leave no monument
More lasting than the sepulchres of kings ;
Although my song-birds fold their failing wings,
And my star tumbles from the firmament ;
Although I may not cheat the discontent
Of Time, who, heedless how a lover sings,
Closes his hand about his throat and clings
Close and clings hard until his life is spent,
I should not heed, if in the hours that run
To dust between my hands, one hour of thee
Flamed like a jewel : so when hot desire
Has passed away, and pleasant youth is done,
A gracious memory may abide with me,
Dreaming of love beside a dying fire.

LAIS.

As one who looking in a wizard's glass
Sees undisturbed phantasmal shapes go by,
Prefiguring the ages yet to die,
When all his time shall lie beneath the grass,
So should I wait and watch your lovers pass,
If I were wise, and never waste a sigh,
Like children for the moon within the sky,
Or hope to be your lover, golden lass.
Your loves are like the shadows on a stream,
Which, living by the favour of the sun,
For that bright hour a brief existence bear;
But with the hidden sun they cease to seem,
And all unchanged the wanton waters run,
As if Love's shade had never fallen there.

TEMPUS EDAX.

HAVE you no pity? Then I turn to Time,
Knowing that in the hollow of his hand,
After some years have spent their shifting sands,
Lies such revenge as shall outpay your crime ;
For Eld, that's skilled most harshly to begrime
All lovely things, your fair can scarce withstand.
So must the beauty fade that could command
The love that lives in my dishonoured rhyme ;
Then when old age has clung you, taking hold
More close than lovers' arms ; when never more
Come kisses on those lips that lose their glow ;
Then while you sorrow for your hair's lost gold,
And that lost seal of grace your body bore,
Think of my name, that loved you long ago.

ARCADIAN.

His surely is a happy lot who dwells
In pleasant pastures far removed from town,
Whose life from sunrise till the sun goes down
The same unchanging peaceful story tells ;
Deep in the rustic lore of fleecy fells,
Proud of the harvest he himself has sown,
The spreading meadows that his hands have mown,
And the great cattle that he buys and sells.
For whom the placid night brings slumber sweet,
Stirred by no sound of any dancing feet,
Lit by no light of any laughing eyes,
Whose quiet days unmoved by vain desire,
From summer's sunlight to the winter's fire,
Creep slowly on, until at last he dies.

ELEUTHEROMANIA.

26 MESSIDOR.

THAT you indeed are with us in some things
Touches us not ; keep thou thy honeyed speech
For love and ladies' praise, nor think to preach
At her whose banners bear the blood of kings.
The minstrel of the red-capped goddess sings
The burden of Marseilles, the best to teach
Democracy with hundred hands to reach
At any throne where any tyrant clings.
We keep our feast of pikes, our sterner feast,
That second rain-month day when Capet died ;
But most the Revolution loves to-day,
This happy day, when in the startled East
The fair sun Freedom burnt in heaven's side,
Flaming from where the fatal prison lay.

ADAM LUX.

WHEN Charlotte Corday journeyed towards the dead
For slaying him she deemed her country's foe,
Through all the angry crowd that watched her go
To that ill place, by frequent blood stained red,
One man, who looked his last on that fair head,
Unshamed as yet by any headsman's blow,
Felt all the currents of his being flow
The quicker for the girl whose life was shed.
Seeing and loving, to like end he came—
Lived but to praise her dead, and praising died
The self-same death of not inglorious shame.
O Adam Lux, thus seeking thy soul's bride
Across the stretch of that ensanguined tide,
High with Love's martyrs let me write thy name.

AN ANGEL BY CIMABUE.

O Cimabue's angel, lowliest
At the right elbow of Madonna's chair,
I long have loved your russet curling hair,
The tender pressure of each girlish breast
On the soft raiment : what among the blest
Have you to do, whose melancholy air,
Scornful in part, and partly of despair,
Says Heaven is good, but surely Earth is best ?
You should have played your part, and not the least,
With those that worshipped Venus long ago ;
That red voluptuous mouth was made to blow
The double pipes at some Athenian feast
Of revel, till the cocks began to crow,
And scarlet sunrise hurried through the East.

LOVE'S LABOUR LOST.

To-night Navarre lays down his crown; to-night
His mimic kingdom withers into air;
No more his rule wins honour anywhere,
And none do homage when he comes in sight;.
No more his merry company delight
In scheming how to break the oaths they swear;
No more they whisper love to ladies fair,
Who come from France to put their vows to flight.
Farewell, Dumain. Lord Longaville, farewell.
And you, Berowne, the jesting slave of love,
Take this farewell from yester evening's king.
Love while you may, nor let your lips rebel
Against the power which makes a woman's glove
The symbol of our highest worshipping.

DEATH.

Out of the air, and exiled from the sun,
Stranger to beauty, stripped of all delight
That lies between the morning and the night,
Of each new day in which our sands may run ;
Farewell to all fair women—everyone
That we have loved, farewell the eyes so bright.
Farewell the lips so sweet to kiss, the light
Hid in their hair, the love now all undone :
Out of the cold, the sorrow, the regret,
The waste despair of hoping against hope,
The dreams too harshly wakened, out of pain ;
Far from the tortures of a love beset
With sorrows, from the darkness where we grope,
Into—alas ! this question ask in vain.

A S R A E L.

FAREWELL to youth, farewell to that which makes
Youth seem so fair; the ignorance of death,
And the brief hour in which we still draw breath,
Unknown while happy childhood sleeps and wakes,
Unknown until that angel comes who breaks
With pitiless hands to-day from yesterday;
For with the human life he bears away,
How much beside the gloomy angel takes!
All hope, all gladness wither in that hour
When first the rudely startled soul is taught
The law of death's inexorable power;
All hope, all gladness wither like a flower;
The sun deserts the sky, and earth is naught
But the chill grave upon whose edge we cower.

THE YEAR'S ANGELS.

OUT watching all alone the dying year
I sudden saw two forms before me stand,
One like an angel bearing in its hand
Such lily-flowers as to the saints are dear;
The other was a shapeless thing of fear,
A dusky vision on whose brow the brand
Of vile old age seemed writ by God's command,
Of whom I wondering asked, 'What do ye here?'
To whom the angel answered, 'Woe is me,
I am your hopes—I am what might have been.
Look on my face, and as you look lament.'
Then that foul other, smiling terribly,
' As in this bright one thou thy hopes hast seen,
Now look on me and learn their fulfilment.'

LOVE'S ENVY.

I AM envious of the wind
When it blows
Kisses to you, oh my fair!

I am envious of the rose
That you bind
In the tresses of your hair.

I am envious of your glove,
Or your fan,
Or the jewel at your breast.

But I envy most the man
Whom you love
For the passing moment best.

TRIOLET.

Lo, my heart so sound asleep !
Lady, will you wake it ?
For lost love I used to weep,
Now my heart is sound asleep.
If it once were yours to keep,
I fear you'd break it.
Lo, my heart so sound asleep !
Lady, will you wake it ?

PYRRHA.

(AFTER HORACE.)

WHAT dainty lover steeped in scented air
Among the roses scattered everywhere,
Shall woo you, Pyrrha, in the grateful cave?
Tell me for whom you bind your yellow hair

Simple in neatness? Ah! how often he
Shall learn to weep for your fidelity
And the changed gods, and wondering behold
How the black breezes rouse the writhing sea!

Alas, poor fool! whose fond and faithful mind
Believes you all his own, and always kind—
Yea, deems you purer than the purest gold,
Who are as false and fleeting as the wind.

Most wretched he to whom untried you shine;
My votive tablet on the wall divine
Proclaims for me that long ago I gave
My dripping garments to the Sea-God's shrine.

THE GODS OF HELLAS.

THE GODS OF HELLAS.

The gods are all forgotten long ago—
The merry gods to whom the Grecians prayed
In those soft words so honey-sweet to flow
Like some rare vintage that for long has stayed
Deep hidden in some happy earthen jar,
Whose ruddy grapes were ripely grown beneath some
      fortunate star.

They have gone hence and left us, floated out
Over the pallid ocean of the sky,
Into those purpling clouds that cling about
The setting splendour of the sun and lie
Upon the edge of plain or sea, unfurled
To the dim shapes of stately gods who ruled an elder
      world.

But ye who pity these poor deities
Whose temples long have tumbled to the earth,
Who from their groves and happy summer seas
Have fled, and left no echo of their mirth,
Pour a libation out to every one
Of the immortal gods who long ago are dead and
      gone.

Although for us the gods are never dead—
For us who, in the yellowing wastes of dawn,
Still see Aurora hasten from her bed—
For us who hear on every upland lawn
The pipings of God Pan upon the breeze,
And see the merry Satyrs chase the Dryads through the
      trees.

And surely when the summer clothes the wold
With gaudy grasses and a world of flowers,
We may believe that Saturn's age of gold
Has come again, and the delightful hours
May pass like comely maidens on their way
About the flaming chariot of the glorious god of day.

In such an hour upon some woodland hill
Lapped in a lazy leisure we may lie,
And dream that Grecian gods inhabit still
The coloured temples of the shifting sky,
Still hearken with some pity to our sighs,
And watch our mortal grief and joy with kindly death-
      less eyes.

They are not dead, the joyous gods of Greece,
A Pan endures where any green thing grows;
Within their hills the Oreads sleep in peace;
The Naiads float where any river flows;
The Dryads linger in each haunted wood;
And still Poseidon and the Nereids rule the writhing
      flood:

And in the evening clouds about the sky
You may behold the shapes of ancient gods.
Can you not see great Ares sweeping by?
And in yon storm-rack Zeus the saviour nods
His curls ambrosial; in that vapour, see,
The fiery steeds of Dis bear off Persephone!

Hail, heavenly Hera, floating down the wind,
Borne by thy gaudy birds, the Argus-eyed!
Now that the gods are banished, do you find
That Zeus remains more faithful by thy side,
Than when of old his uncontrolled desire
On half the heroes of the world bestowed a heavenly
        sire?

Great Pan, the laughing fountains and the edges
Of ancient rivers are thy altars still;
And where the wind makes sport among the sedges
Thy pleasant pipings of lost Syrinx fill
The hollow groves and mossy mountain ledges:
And so we find old Arcady between our leafy hedges.

God of the gardens, lord of Lampsacus,
Grinning with half shut eyes against the sun
Although the world has laughed and left you thus
With desolate altars, where sad ivies run,
Yet, while the Queen of Love finds worshippers,
Be well assured your horde of slaves shall aye out-
        number hers.

Wing-footed Hermes, cunning king of thieves,
Whose duty 'twas to herald down to hell
The ghosts more thick than winter-scattered leaves,
Say, hast thou led the shapes of gods as well?
Hast thou, thyself a shade, been forced to float
Across the muddy waves of Styx in Charon's creaking
            boat?

Archer Apollo, young in the world's age,
Come with the sunshine in your face and hair!
You served Admetus once; ah! with what wage
Will ye serve us, whose summer fields are fair,
And fair our meadows and our wood-clad hills,
And fair our babbling rivers as the old Castalian rills?

O golden lord of sunlight, goodliest
Of all thy heavenly fellows, where are they,
Calliope, Euterpe, and the rest
Of thy nine maidens? Have they lost their way
To old Parnassus, where the trembling trees
Give to the winds the echo of your ancient melodies?

Where is thy sister Artemis to-day,
Lyric Apollo? Do her white feet run
Down the green track to bring the stag to bay
In some unknown-of forest, where the sun
Shines on the shapes of deathless deities,
That wander in eternal youth among eternal trees?

Surely of moonlit nights the Parthenon
Beholds Athene, and the broad white brows
Of Pallas bent in godlike grief upon
Her much beloved Piræus, where the prows
Of all the nations cluster as of old,
When she was throned in solemn pride of ivory and
    gold.

Surely about that ghostly hour when dawn
Creeps through the sky and stares on Salamis,
The ghosts come thick from each Elysian lawn,
And from the hollow flowerless fields of Dis,
And wend their way from the still town in pairs
To greet their goddess at the head of holy temple
    stairs.

Those comely youths with lissom limbs that ride
Around thy storied frieze, O Virginal!
Those glorious girls for whom their lovers sighed
What time they went upon thy festival,
Bearing thy yellow garment softly spun
In token that another year of jocund life was run.

Once more the noisy gaily coloured crowd
People thy holy courts with many a gift ;
Once more the choral voices, rising loud
In clear triumphant tuneful union, lift
Thy holy praises to the heedless sky.
O goddess, these are dead and gone who thought not
    thou couldst die !

Down on the hill the long-deserted stage
Is thronged with changing shadows ; sure I see
The tortured Titan brave Olympian rage,
And Œdipus bewail his misery
By white Colonos, from whose olive trees
Thick haunting nightingales make moan to every
      wandering breeze.

Medea, with love's ruin in her heart,
Calls to her young with cruel Colchian breath ;
The great good-humoured giant takes the part
Of the true woman and o'ermasters death ;
And lo, from seat to seat runs ghostly mirth,
While Socrates in basket swings between the heaven
      and earth!

O Dionysus, gladdest-hearted god,
Do not the purple vineyards hold you still?
Do you not rule us with your tendrilled rod,
And the soft juices that defeat the will,
From any heed of cruel hours that creep
Away in fancies brighter than the dreams of poppied
      sleep?

For every man to whom the subtle fire
Gives an unreal lordship of the earth,
And feigned accordance of his heart's desire—
The love of woman or what nobler worth
His heart most hungers after—each of these
Adds one more loyal worshipper to all your votaries.

No more the dappled leopards draw thy car
Adown the noisy flower-sown street; no more
Some baby Bacchus on a giant jar,
By jolly vine-clad Satyrs lifted o'er
The heads of all the laughing people, wields
His little thyrsus in the praise of him the vineyard
      yields.

Perchance on summer evenings calm and still,
You sit with Ariadne by your side
On the soft slope of some Arcadian hill,
Singing and drinking of the purple tide,
Crushed beneath sunburnt feet with merry noise
Of laughter and of rustic song from brown-skinned
      girls and boys.

No more the laughing girls, with bright limbs bare
To all the kisses of the wind and sun,
With twisted ivy in their tumbled hair,
And girt with skins of gaudy leopards, run
About thy jocund car, and leap and bound
To music of the double pipes and clashing cymbals
      sound.

But we, while drinking of the earth's best blood
That glows and trembles in some well-crowned cup,
Even as we bend to the delightful flood,
Think of thy name, an l once again fill up,
With shouts of 'Io Bacchus, evoe !
Hail thou that teachest men how best to laugh the
      world away !'

For if perchance some woman's loveliness
Dazzle more surely than the noontide sun,
Would we forget the lips we long to press,
And may not—watch ye how the red drops run
Into some spacious goblet over-crowned ;
There drink till all your dreams in that Lethean stream
       are drowned.

For while you drink of that immortal juice,
All hopes seem idle, idle all desire,
And lordship of the earth of little use,
And love no better than a burnt-out fire,
Whilst thou, Lyæan, in the guise of wine
Slipst through our veins, and makest us seem for that
       bright hour divine.

Lo, the unfettered fancy floats away
Into the far fantastic land of dreams,
Where the pure sunlight of a warmer day
Gilds deathless meadows and immortal streams—
The true Elysian fields, the Fortunate Isles,
Where women aye are young, and kind, and ever full
       of smiles !

O Dionysus, when the southern wind
Blows softly through the vineyards, sure thy breath
Is mingled with its course and makes it kind,
That when the grapes are carried to their death
In the great winepress such sweet juice shall flow
As gods and mighty heroes cupped in Hellas long ago !

Oh for one beaker of those wondrous wines,
Tides of a thousand vineyards cool and clear,
Whose names, like music, linger in the lines
Of some forgotten Grecian singer dear
To all the muses, and most dear to thee,
Thou merriest god that ever trod the land or sailed
      the sea !

Those glorious liquors of the Grecian valleys,
Whose grapes were gathered when the south wind
      blows
Its softest kisses through the narrow alleys
Of sunny vineyards where the ripe grape glows,
Waiting the moment to be pluckt and pressed
To that dark stream, its drinkers blessing, by its drinkers
      blessed.

High Homer's Chian, and the rare perfume
Of honeyed Thasian ; Saprian that closes
Within its scented stream the triple bloom
Of hyacinths and violets and roses ;
True Psithian nectar ; Rhodian and Mendæan,
Loved by the gods and by all men who raised the Io
      pæan.

And then the glorious Lesbian, loved the best
Of all the vineyards of the antique earth ;
O fortunate island, and thus doubly blessed,
That to such wine and to such songs gave birth,
The sweetest and the saddest ever sung
To happy mortal ears by any hapless mortal tongue !

Pramnian, the vintage of the holy vine
That grows in fishful Icarus they say,
Was of all juices the most wondrous wine
For strength to drive all angry thoughts away :
But all these streams are long ago drunk up,
And we must thirst in vain for drink that crowned an
        ancient cup.

O glorious goddess, if my prayer could reach
To the dark hollow of thy haunted hill,
Or haply find thee by the yellow beach
Of some lone Grecian island where the still
Blue waters tell the tale that Sappho told,
And know to-day no gods except the merry gods of old,

Would you not hear me, even as long ago
You heard the lovelorn girl of Mytilene
Cry for the faithless fool she worshipped so?
Would you not hear and pity, O my queen !
Give me my love, if you have still the power
Which gave the boy of Ida her of womenkind the
    · flower ?

Sometimes before your image, which the hand
Of some Greek sculptor fashioned for a shrine
For Grecian lovers, I have dared to stand,
Praying and dreaming that the lips divine
Parted and smiled in pity for my pain.
O helper of unhappy men, be helper once again !

O lover, tortured with a vain desire
For some fair woman, till in every place
You seek your wandering star, and come no nigher
The splendour of that fair Olympian face
And purple mouth, of which one single kiss
Were worth whole cycles, age on age, of barren loveless
      bliss !

You are the servant of the Cyprian Queen !
No less than those who by the silver flood,
Or in some temple garden evergreen,
Implored her by Adonis' dabbled blood,
And for her many mortal lovers' sake,
To pity lips that wait unkissed, and hungry hearts that
      ache.

O Lady and O Queen ! be sure of this,
That if my homage at thy altar-shrine
Could give me up one woman's lips to kiss,
Could make the girl I love but one hour mine,
No one of all thy singers of old time
Could hymn thy praises with more loyal or more
      loving rhyme !

THE END.

BILLING AND SONS, PRINTERS, GUILDFORD AND LONDON.

CHATTO & WINDUS'S
LIST OF BOOKS.

About.—The Fellah: An Egyptian Novel. By EDMOND ABOUT. Translated by Sir RANDAL ROBERTS. Post 8vo, illustrated boards, 2s. ; cloth limp, 2s. 6d.

Adams (W. Davenport), Works by:

A Dictionary of the Drama. Being a comprehensive Guide to the Plays, Playwrights, Players, and Playhouses of the United Kingdom and America, from the Earliest to the Present Times. Crown 8vo, half-bound, 12s. 6d. [*In preparation.*

Latter-Day Lyrics. Edited by W. DAVENPORT ADAMS. Post 8vo, cloth limp, 2s 6d.

Quips and Quiddities. Selected by W. DAVENPORT ADAMS. Post 8vo, cloth limp, 2s. 6d.

Advertising, A History of, from the Earliest Times. Illustrated by Anecdotes, Curious Specimens, and Notices of Successful Advertisers. By HENRY SAMPSON. Crown 8vo, with Coloured Frontispiece and Illustrations, cloth gilt, 7s. 6d.

Agony Column (The) of "The Times," from 1800 to 1870. Edited, with an Introduction, by ALICE CLAY. Post 8vo, cloth limp, 2s. 6d.

Aide (Hamilton), Works by:

Carr of Carrlyon. Post 8vo, illustrated boards, 2s.

Confidences. Post 8vo, illustrated boards, 2s.

Alexander (Mrs.).—Maid, Wife, or Widow? A Romance. By Mrs. ALEXANDER. Post 8vo, illustrated boards, 2s. ; cr. 8vo, cloth extra, 3s. 6d.

Allen (Grant), Works by:

Colin Clout's Calendar. Crown 8vo, cloth extra, 6s.

The Evolutionist at Large. Crown 8vo, cloth extra, 6s.

Vignettes from Nature. Crown 8vo, cloth extra, 6s.

Architectural Styles, A Handbook of. Translated from the German of A. ROSENGARTEN, by W. COLLETT-SANDARS. Crown 8vo, cloth extra, with 639 Illustrations, 7s. 6d.

Art (The) of Amusing: A Collection of Graceful Arts, Games, Tricks, Puzzles, and Charades. By FRANK BELLEW. With 300 Illustrations. Cr. 8vo, cloth extra, 4s. 6d.

Artemus Ward:

Artemus Ward's Works: The Works of CHARLES FARRER BROWNE, better known as ARTEMUS WARD. With Portrait and Facsimile. Crown 8vo, cloth extra, 7s. 6d.

Artemus Ward's Lecture on the Mormons. With 32 Illustrations. Edited, with Preface, by EDWARD P. HINGSTON. Crown 8vo, 6d

The Genial Showman: Life and Adventures of Artemus Ward. By EDWARD P. HINGSTON. With a Frontispiece. Crown 8vo, cloth extra, 3s. 6d.

Ashton (John), Works by :

A History of the Chap Books of the Eighteenth Century. With nearly 400 Illustrations, engraved in fac-simile of the originals. Crown 8vo, cloth extra, 7s. 6d.

Social Life in the Reign of Queen Anne. Taken from Original Sources. With nearly One Hundred Illustrations. New and cheaper Edition, crown 8vo, cloth extra, 7s. 6d.

Humour, Wit, and Satire of the Seventeenth Century. With nearly 100 Illustrations. Crown 8vo, cloth extra, 7s. 6d. One Hundred large-paper copies (only seventy-five of them for sale) will be carefully printed on hand-made paper, crown 4to, parchment boards, price 42s. Early application must be made for these.   [*In preparation.*

Ballad History (The) of England By W. C. BENNETT. Post 8vo, cloth limp, 2s.

Balzac's "Comedie Humaine" and its Author. With Translations by H. H. WALKER. Post 8vo, cloth limp, 2s. 6d.

Bankers, A Handbook of London; together with Lists of Bankers from 1677. By F. G. HILTON PRICE. Crown 8vo, cloth extra, 7s. 6d.

Bardsley (Rev. C.W.), Works by :

English Surnames: Their Sources and Significations. Crown 8vo, cloth extra, 7s. 6d.

Curiosities of Puritan Nomenclature. Crown 8vo, cloth extra, 7s. 6d.

Bartholomew Fair, Memoirs of. By HENRY MORLEY. A New Edition, with One Hundred Illustrations. Crown 8vo, cloth extra, 7s. 6d.

Beauchamp. — Grantley Grange: A Novel. By SHELSLEY BEAUCHAMP. Post 8vo, illustrated boards, 2s.

Beautiful Pictures by British Artists: A Gathering of Favourites from our Picture Galleries. In Two Series. All engraved on Steel in the highest style of Art. Edited, with Notices of the Artists, by SYDNEY ARMYTAGE, M.A. Imperial 4to, cloth extra, gilt and gilt edges, 21s. per Vol.

Bechstein. — As Pretty as Seven, and other German Stories. Collected by LUDWIG BECHSTEIN. With Additional Tales by the Brothers GRIMM, and 100 Illusts. by RICHTER. Small 4to, green and gold, 6s. 6d.; gilt edges, 7s. 6d.

Beerbohm. — Wanderings in Patagonia; or, Life among the Ostrich Hunters. By JULIUS BEERBOHM. With Illusts. Crown 8vo, cloth extra, 3s. 6d.

Belgravia for 1883. One Shilling Monthly, Illustrated.—"Maid of Athens," JUSTIN McCARTHY's New Serial Story, Illustrated by FRED. BARNARD, was begun in the JANUARY Number of BELGRAVIA, which Number contained also the First Portion of a Story in Three Parts, by OUIDA, entitled "Frescoes;" the continuation of WILKIE COLLINS's Novel, "Heart and Science;" a further instalment of Mrs. ALEXANDER's Novel, "The Admiral's Ward;" and other Matters of Interest.

** *Now ready, the Volume for Nov.* 1882 *to* FEBRUARY 1883 *(which includes the* BELGRAVIA ANNUAL*), cloth extra, gilt edges, 7s. 6d.; Cases for binding Volumes, 2s. each.*

Belgravia Holiday Number, written by the well-known Authors who have been so long associated with the Magazine, will be published as usual in July.

Besant (Walter) and James Rice, Novels by. Each in post 8vo, illustrated boards, 2s.; cloth limp, 2s. 6d.; or crown 8vo, cloth extra, 3s. 6d.

Ready-Money Mortiboy.

With Harp and Crown.

This Son of Vulcan.

My Little Girl.

The Case of Mr. Lucraft.

The Golden Butterfly.

By Celia's Arbour.

The Monks of Thelema.

'Twas in Trafalgar's Bay.

The Seamy Side.

The Ten Years' Tenant.

The Chaplain of the Fleet.

Besant (Walter), Novels by :

All Sorts and Conditions of Men: An Impossible Story. With Illustrations by FRED. BARNARD. Crown 8vo, cloth extra, 3s. 6d.

The Captains' Room, &c. Three Vols., crown 8vo, 31s. 6d.

Birthday Book.—The Starry Heavens: A Poetical Birthday Book. Square 8vo, handsomely bound in cloth, 3s. 6d. [*In preparation.*

Birthday Flowers: Their Language and Legends. By W. J. GORDON. Beautifully Illustrated in Colours by VIOLA BOUGHTON. In illuminated cover, crown 4to, 6s. [*Shortly.*

Blackburn's (Henry) Art Handbooks. Demy 8vo, Illustrated, uniform in size for binding.

Academy Notes, separate years, from 1875 to 1882, each 1s.

Academy Notes, 1883. With Illustrations. 1s.

Academy Notes, 1375-79. Complete in One Volume, with nearly 600 Illustrations in Facsimile. Demy 8vo, cloth limp, 6s.

Grosvenor Notes, 1877. 6d.

Grosvenor Notes, separate years, from 1878 to 1882, each 1s.

Grosvenor Notes, 1883. With Illustrations. 1s.

Grosvenor Notes, 1877-82. With upwards of 300 Illustrations. Demy 8vo, cloth limp, 6s.

Pictures at South Kensington. With 70 Illustrations. 1s.

The English Pictures at the National Gallery. 114 Illustrations. 1s.

The Old Masters at the National Gallery. 128 Illustrations. 1s. 6d.

A Complete Illustrated Catalogue to the National Gallery. With Notes by H. BLACKBURN, and 242 Illusts. Demy 8vo, cloth limp, 3s.

The Paris Salon, 1883. With 400 full-page Illustrations. Edited by F. G. DUMAS. (English Edition.) Demy 8vo, 3s.

At the Paris Salon. Sixteen large Plates, printed in facsimile of the Artists' Drawings, in two tints. Edited by F. G. DUMAS. Large folio, 1s. [*Immediately.*

The Art Annual. Edited by F. G. DUMAS. With 250 full-page Illusts. Demy 8vo, 3s. 6d.

Blake (William): Etchings from his Works. By W. B. SCOTT. With descriptive Text. Folio, half-bound boards, India Proofs, 21s.

Boccaccio's Decameron: or, Ten Days' Entertainment. Translated into English, with an Introduction by THOMAS WRIGHT, F.S.A. With Portrait, and STOTHARD'S beautiful Copperplates. Cr. 8vo, cloth extra, gilt, 7s. 6d.

Bowers'(G.) Hunting Sketches:

Canters in Crampshire. Oblong 4to, half-bound boards, 21s.

Leaves from a Hunting Journal. Coloured in facsimile of the originals. Oblong 4to, half-bound, 21s.

Boyle (Frederick), Works by:

Camp Notes: Stories of Sport and Adventure in Asia, Africa, and America. Crown 8vo, cloth extra, 3s. 6d.; post 8vo, illustrated bds., 2s.

Savage Life. Crown 8vo, cloth extra, 3s. 6d.; post 8vo, illustrated bds., 2s.

Brand's Observations on Popular Antiquities, chiefly Illustrating the Origin of our Vulgar Customs, Ceremonies, and Superstitions. With the Additions of Sir HENRY ELLIS. Crown 8vo, cloth extra, gilt, with numerous Illustrations, 7s. 6d.

Bret Harte, Works by:

Bret Harte's Collected Works. Arranged and Revised by the Author. Complete in Five Vols., crown 8vo, cloth extra, 6s. each.

Vol. I. COMPLETE POETICAL AND DRAMATIC WORKS. With Steel Plate Portrait, and an Introduction by the Author.

Vol. II. EARLIER PAPERS—LUCK OF ROARING CAMP, and other Sketches —BOHEMIAN PAPERS — SPANISH AND AMERICAN LEGENDS.

Vol. III. TALES OF THE ARGONAUTS —EASTERN SKETCHES.

Vol. IV. GABRIEL CONROY.

Vol. V. STORIES — CONDENSED NOVELS, &c.

The Select Works of Bret Harte, in Prose and Poetry. With Introductory Essay by J. M. BELLEW, Portrait of the Author, and 50 Illustrations. Crown 8vo, cloth extra, 7s. 6d.

Gabriel Conroy: A Novel. Post 8vo, illustrated boards, 2s.

An Heiress of Red Dog, and other Stories. Post 8vo, illustrated boards, 2s.; cloth limp, 2s. 6d.

The Twins of Table Mountain. Fcap. 8vo, picture cover, 1s.; crown 8vo, cloth extra, 3s. 6d.

The Luck of Roaring Camp, and other Sketches. Post 8vo, illustrated boards, 2s.

Jeff Briggs's Love Story. Fcap. 8vo, picture cover, 1s.; cloth extra, 2s. 6d.

Flip. Post 8vo, illustrated boards, 2s.; cloth limp, 2s. 6d.

Brewer (Rev. Dr.), Works by :

The Reader's Handbook of Allusions, References, Plots, and Stories. Third Edition, revised throughout, with a New Appendix, containing a COMPLETE ENGLISH BIBLIOGRAPHY. Crown 8vo, 1,400 pages, cloth extra, 7s. 6d

A Dictionary of Miracles: Imitative, Realistic, and Dogmatic. Crown 8vo, cloth extra, 7s. 6d   [*In preparation.*

Buchanan's (Robert) Works :

Ballads of Life, Love, and Humour. With a Frontispiece by ARTHUR HUGHES. Crown 8vo, cloth extra, 6s.

Selected Poems of Robert Buchanan. With Frontispiece by T. DALZIEL. Crown 8vo, cloth extra, 6s.

Undertones. Crown 8vo, cloth extra, 6s.

London Poems. Crown 8vo, cloth extra, 6s.

The Book of Orm. Crown 8vo, cloth extra, 6s.

White Rose and Red: A Love Story. Crown 8vo, cloth extra, 6s.

Idyllic and Legends of Inverburn. Crown 8vo, cloth extra, 6s.

St. Abe and his Seven Wives: A Tale of Salt Lake City. With a Frontispiece by A. B. HOUGHTON. Crown 8vo, cloth extra, 5s.

The Hebrid Isles: Wanderings in the Land of Lorne and the Outer Hebrides. With Frontispiece by W. SMALL. Crown 8vo, cloth extra, 6s.

Selections from the Prose Writings of Robert Buchanan. Crown 8vo, cloth extra, 6s.   [*Shortly.*

Robert Buchanan's Complete Poetical Works. Crown 8vo, cloth extra, 7s. 6d.   [*In preparation.*

The Shadow of the Sword: A Romance. Crown 8vo, cloth extra, 3s. 6d.; post 8vo, illust. boards, 2s.

A Child of Nature: A Romance. With a Frontispiece. Crown 8vo, cloth extra, 3s. 6d.; post 8vo, illustrated boards, 2s.

God and the Man: A Romance. With Illustrations by FRED. BARNARD. Crown 8vo, cloth extra, 3s. 6d.

The Martyrdom of Madeline: A Romance. With a Frontispiece by A. W. COOPER. Crown 8vo, cloth extra, 3s. 6d.

Love Me for Ever. With a Frontispiece by P. MACNAB. Crown 8vo, cloth extra, 3s. 6d.

Annan Water: A Romance. Three Vols., cr. 8vo, 31s. 6d.   [*Immediately.*

Brewster (Sir David), Works by :

More Worlds than One: The Creed of the Philosopher and the Hope of the Christian. With Plates. Post 8vo, cloth extra, 4s. 6d.

The Martyrs of Science: Lives of GALILEO, TYCHO BRAHE, and KEPLER. With Portraits. Post 8vo, cloth extra, 4s. 6d.

Letters on Natural Magic. A New Edition, with numerous Illustrations, and Chapters on the Being and Faculties of Man, and Additional Phenomena of Natural Magic, by J. A. SMITH. Post 8vo, cloth extra, 4s. 6d.

Brillat-Savarin.—Gastronomy as a Fine Art. By BRILLAT-SAVARIN. Translated by R. E. ANDERSON, M.A. Post 8vo, cloth limp, 2s. 6d.

Burnett (Mrs.), Novels by :

Surly Tim, and other Stories. Post 8vo, illustrated boards, 2s.

Kathleen Mavourneen. Fcap. 8vo, picture cover, 1s.

Lindsay's Luck. Fcap. 8vo, picture cover, 1s.

Pretty Polly Pemberton. Fcap. 8vo, picture cover, 1s.

Burton (Robert):

The Anatomy of Melancholy. A New Edition, complete, corrected and enriched by Translations of the Classical Extracts. Demy 8vo, cloth extra, 7s. 6d.

Melancholy Anatomised: Being an Abridgment, for popular use, of BURTON'S ANATOMY OF MELANCHOLY. Post 8vo, cloth limp, 2s. 6d.

Burton (Captain), Works by :

To the Gold Coast for Gold: A Personal Narrative. By RICHARD F. BURTON and VERNEY LOVETT CAMERON. With Maps and Frontispiece. Two Vols., crown 8vo, cloth extra, 21s.

The Book of the Sword: Being a History of the Sword and its Use in all Countries, from the Earliest Times. By RICHARD F. BURTON. With over 400 Illustrations. Square 8vo, cloth extra, 25s. [*In preparation.*

Bunyan's Pilgrim's Progress. Edited by Rev. T. SCOTT. With 17 beautiful Steel Plates by STOTHARD, engraved by GOODALL; and numerous Woodcuts. Crown 8vo, cloth extra, gilt, 7s. 6d.

Byron (Lord):

Byron's **Letters and Journals.** With Notices of his Life. By THOMAS MOORE. A Reprint of the Original Edition, newly revised, with Twelve full-page Plates. Crown 8vo, cloth extra, gilt, **7s. 6d.**

Byron's **Don Juan.** Complete in One Vol., post 8vo, cloth limp, **2s.**

Cameron (Commander) and Captain Burton.—**To the Gold Coast for Gold:** A Personal Narrative. By RICHARD F. BURTON and VERNEY LOVETT CAMERON. With Frontispiece and Maps. Two Vols., crown 8vo, cloth extra, **21s.**

Cameron (Mrs. H. Lovett). Novels by:

Juliet's **Guardian.** Post 8vo, illustrated boards, **2s.**; crown 8vo, cloth extra, **3s. 6d.**

Deceivers **Ever.** Post 8vo, illustrated boards, **2s.**; crown 8vo, cloth extra, **3s. 6d.**

Campbell.—White and Black: Travels in the United States. By Sir GEORGE CAMPBELL, M.P. Demy 8vo, cloth extra, **14s.**

Carlyle (Thomas):

Thomas Carlyle: **Letters and Re collections.** By MONCURE D. CONWAY, M.A. Crown 8vo, cloth extra, with Illustrations, **6s.**

On the **Choice of Books.** By THOMAS CARLYLE. With a Life of the Author by R. H. SHEPHERD. New and Revised Edition, post 8vo, cloth extra, Illustrated, **1s. 6d.**

The **Correspondence of Thomas Carlyle and Ralph Waldo Emerson,** 1834 to 1872. Edited by CHARLES ELIOT NORTON. With Portraits. Two Vols., crown 8vo, cloth extra, **24s.**

Century (A) of Dishonour: A Sketch of the United States Government's Dealings with some of the Indian Tribes. Crown 8vo, cloth extra, **7s. 6d.**

Chapman's (George) Works: Vol. I. contains the Plays complete, including the doubtful ones. Vol. II., the Poems and Minor Translations, with an Introductory Essay by ALGERNON CHARLES SWINBURNE. Vol. III., the Translations of the Iliad and Odyssey. Three Vols., crown 8vo, cloth extra, **18s.**; or separately, **6s. each.**

Chatto & Jackson.—A Treatise on Wood Engraving, Historical and Practical. By WM. ANDREW CHATTO and JOHN JACKSON. With an Additional Chapter by HENRY G. BOHN; and 450 fine Illustrations. A Reprint of the last Revised Edition, Large 4to, half-bound, **28s.**

Chaucer:

Chaucer for Children: A Golden Key. By Mrs. H. R. HAWEIS. With Eight Coloured Pictures and numerous Woodcuts by the Author. New Ed., small 4to, cloth extra, **6s.**

Chaucer for Schools. By Mrs. H. R. HAWEIS. Demy 8vo, cloth limp, **2s. 6d.**

Cobban.—The Cure of Souls: A Story. By J. MACLAREN COBBAN. Post 8vo, illustrated boards, **2s.**

Collins (C. Allston).—The Bar Sinister: A Story. By C. ALLSTON COLLINS. Post 8vo, illustrated boards, **2s.**

Collins (Mortimer & Frances), Novels by:

Sweet and **Twenty.** Post 8vo, illustrated boards, **2s.**

Frances. Post 8vo, illust. bds., **2s.**

Blacksmith and **Scholar.** Post 8vo, illustrated boards, **2s.**; crown 8vo, cloth extra, **3s. 6d.**

The Village **Comedy.** Post 8vo, illust. boards, **2s.**; cr. 8vo, cloth extra, **3s. 6d.**

You Play Me **False.** Post 8vo, illust. boards, **2s.**; cr. 8vo, cloth extra, **3s. 6d.**

Collins (Mortimer), Novels by:

Sweet Anne **Page.** Post 8vo, illustrated boards, **2s.**; crown 8vo, cloth extra, **3s. 6d.**

Transmigration. Post 8vo, illustrated boards, **2s.**; crown 8vo, cloth extra, **3s. 6d.**

From Midnight to **Midnight.** Post 8vo, illustrated boards, **2s.**; crown 8vo, cloth extra, **3s. 6d.**

A Fight with **Fortune.** Post 8vo, illustrated boards, **2s.**

Colman's Humorous Works: "Broad Grins," "My Nightgown and Slippers," and other Humorous Works, Prose and Poetical, of GEORGE COLMAN. With Life by G. B. BUCKSTONE, and Frontispiece by HOGARTH. Crown 8vo, cloth extra, gilt, **7s. 6d.**

Collins (Wilkie), Novels by.

Each post 8vo, illustrated boards, 2s; cloth limp, 2s. 6d.; or crown 8vo, cloth extra, Illustrated, 3s. 6d.

Antonina. Illust. by A. Concanen.

Basil. Illustrated by Sir John Gilbert and J. Mahoney.

Hide and Seek. Illustrated by Sir John Gilbert and J. Mahoney.

The Dead Secret. Illustrated by Sir John Gilbert and A. Concanen.

Queen of Hearts. Illustrated by Sir John Gilbert and A. Concanen.

My Miscellanies. With Illustrations by A. Concanen, and a Steel-plate Portrait of Wilkie Collins.

The Woman in White. With Illustrations by Sir John Gilbert and F. A. Fraser.

The Moonstone. With Illustrations by G. Du Maurier and F. A. Fraser.

Man and Wife. Illust. by W. Small.

Poor Miss Finch. Illustrated by G. Du Maurier and Edward Hughes.

Miss or Mrs.? With Illustrations by S. L. Fildes and Henry Woods.

The New Magdalen. Illustrated by G. Du Maurier and C. S. Rands.

The Frozen Deep. Illustrated by G. Du Maurier and J. Mahoney.

The Law and the Lady. Illustrated by S. L. Fildes and Sydney Hall.

The Two Destinies.

The Haunted Hotel. Illustrated by Arthur Hopkins.

The Fallen Leaves.

Jezebel's Daughter.

The Black Robe.

Heart and Science: A Story of the Present Time. Three Vols., crown 8vo, 31s. 6d.

Convalescent Cookery: A

Family Handbook. By Catherine Ryan. Post 8vo, cloth limp, 2s. 6d.

Conway (Moncure D.), Works by:

Demonology and Devil Lore. Two Vols., royal 8vo, with 65 Illusts., 28s.

A Necklace of Stories. Illustrated by W. J. Hennessy. Square 8vo, cloth extra, 6s.

The Wandering Jew. Crown 8vo, cloth extra, 6s.

Thomas Carlyle: Letters and Recollections. With Illustrations. Crown 8vo, cloth extra, 9s.

Cook (Dutton), Works by:

Hours with the Players. With a Steel Plate Frontispiece. New and Cheaper Edit., cr. 8vo, cloth extra, 6s.

Nights at the Play: A View of the English Stage. Two Vols., crown 8vo, cloth extra, 21s.

Leo: A Novel. Post 8vo, illustrated boards, 2s.

Paul Foster's Daughter. Post 8vo, illustrated boards, 2s.; crown 8vo, cloth extra, 3s. 6d. [Shortly.

Copyright. — A Handbook of

English and Foreign Copyright in Literary and Dramatic Works. By Sidney Jerrold, of the Middle Temple, Esq., Barrister-at-Law. Post 8vo, cloth limp, 2s. 6d.

Cornwall.—Popular Romances

of the West of England; or, The Drolls, Traditions, and Superstitions of Old Cornwall. Collected and Edited by Robert Hunt, F.R.S. New and Revised Edition, with Additions, and Two Steel-plate Illustrations by George Cruikshank. Crown 8vo, cloth extra, 7s. 6d.

Creasy.—Memoirs of Eminent

Etonians: with Notices of the Early History of Eton College. By Sir Edward Creasy, Author of "The Fifteen Decisive Battles of the World." Crown 8vo, cloth extra, gilt, with 13 Portraits, 7s. 6d.

Cruikshank (George):

The Comic Almanack. Complete in Two Series: The First from 1835 to 1843; the Second from 1844 to 1853. A Gathering of the Best Humour of Thackeray, Hood, Mayhew, Albert Smith, A'Beckett, Robert Brough, &c. With 2,000 Woodcuts and Steel Engravings by Cruikshank, Hine, Landells, &c. Crown 8vo, cloth gilt, two very thick volumes, 7s. 6d. each.

The Life of George Cruikshank. By Blanchard Jerrold, Author of "The Life of Napoleon III.," &c. With 84 Illustrations. New and Cheaper Edition, enlarged, with Additional Plates, and a very carefully compiled Bibliography. Crown 8vo, cloth extra, 7s. 6d. [Shortly.

Robinson Crusoe. A choicely-printed Edition, with 37 Woodcuts and Two Steel Plates, by George Cruikshank. Crown 8vo, cloth extra, 7s. 6d. A few Large Paper copies, carefully printed on hand-made paper, with India proofs of the Illustrations, price 36s. [In preparation.

Crimes and Punishments. Including a New Translation of Beccaria's "De Delitti e delle Pene." By JAMES ANSON FARRER. Crown 8vo, cloth extra, **6s.**

Cumming.—In the Hebrides. By C. F. GORDON CUMMING, Author of "At Home in Fiji." With Autotype Facsimile and Illustrations. Demy 8vo, cloth extra, **8s. 6d.** [Preparing.

Cussans.—Handbook of Heraldry; with Instructions for Tracing Pedigrees and Deciphering Ancient MSS., &c. By JOHN E. CUSSANS. Entirely New and Revised Edition, illustrated with over 400 Woodcuts and Coloured Plates. Crown 8vo, cloth extra, **7s. 6d.**

Cyples.—Hearts of Gold: A Novel. By WILLIAM CYPLES. Crown 8vo, cloth extra, **3s. 6d.**

Daniel. — Merrie England in the Olden Time. By GEORGE DANIEL. With Illustrations by ROBT. CRUIKSHANK. Crown 8vo, cloth extra, **3s. 6d.**

Daudet.—Port Salvation; or, The Evangelist. By ALPHONSE DAUDET. Translated by C. HARRY MELTZER. Two Vols., post 8vo, **12s.**

Davenant. — What shall my Son be? Hints for Parents on the Choice of a Profession or Trade for their Sons. By FRANCIS DAVENANT, M.A. Post 8vo, cloth limp, **2s. 6d.**

Davies' (Sir John) Complete Poetical Works, including Psalms I. to L. in Verse, and other hitherto Unpublished MSS., for the first time Collected and Edited, with Memorial-Introduction and Notes, by the Rev. A. B. GROSART, D.D. Two Vols., crown 8vo, cloth boards, **12s.**

De Maistre.—A Journey Round My Room. By XAVIER DE MAISTRE. Translated by HENRY ATTWELL. Post 8vo, cloth limp, **2s. 6d.**

Derwent (Leith), Novels by:
Our Lady of Tears. Crown 8vo, cloth extra, **3s. 6d.**; post 8vo, illustrated boards, **2s.** [Shortly.
Circe's Lovers. Three Vols., crown 8vo, **31s. 6d.** [Shortly.

Dickens (Charles), Novels by:
Post 8vo, illustrated boards, **2s.** each.
Sketches by Boz.
The Pickwick Papers.
Oliver Twist.
Nicholas Nickleby.

The Speeches of Charles Dickens. Post 8vo, cloth limp, **2s. 6d.**

Charles Dickens's Speeches, Chronologically Arranged; with a New Life of the Author, and a Bibliographical List of his Published Writings in Prose and Verse, from 1833 to 1883. Crown 8vo, cloth extra, **6s.** [In preparation.

About England with Dickens. By ALFRED RIMMER. With 57 Illustrations by C. A. VANDERHOOF, ALFRED RIMMER, and others. Sq. 8vo, cloth extra, **10s. 6d.**

Dictionaries:

A **Dictionary of Miracles:** Imitative, Realistic, and Dogmatic. By the Rev. E. C. BREWER, LL.D. Crown 8vo, cloth extra, **7s. 6d.** [Preparing.

A **Dictionary of the Drama:** Being a comprehensive Guide to the Plays, Playwrights, Players, and Playhouses of the United Kingdom and America, from the Earliest to the Present Times. By W. DAVENPORT ADAMS. A thick volume, crown 8vo, half-bound, **12s. 6d.** [In preparation.

Familiar Allusions: A Handbook of Miscellaneous Information; including the Names of Celebrated Statues, Paintings, Palaces, Country Seats, Ruins, Churches, Ships, Streets, Clubs, Natural Curiosities, and the like. By WM. A. WHEELER and CHARLES G. WHEELER. Demy 8vo, cloth extra, **7s. 6d.**

The Reader's Handbook of Allusions, References, Plots, and Stories. By the Rev. E. C. BREWER, LL.D. Third Edition, revised throughout, with a New Appendix, containing a Complete English Bibliography. Crown 8vo, 1,400 pages, cloth extra, **7s. 6d.**

Short Sayings of Great Men. With Historical and Explanatory Notes. By SAMUEL A. BENT, M.A. Demy 8vo, cloth extra, **7s. 6d.**

The Slang Dictionary: Etymological, Historical, and Anecdotal. Crown 8vo, cloth extra, **6s. 6d.**

DICTIONARIES, *continued*—

Words, Facts, and Phrases: A Dictionary of Curious, Quaint, and Out-of-the-Way Matters By ELIEZER EDWARDS. Crown 8vo, half-bound, 12s. 6d.

Dobson (W. T.), Works by:

Literary Frivolities, Fancies, Follies, and Frolics. Post 8vo, cloth limp, 2s. 6d.

Poetical Ingenuities and Eccentricities. Post 8vo, cloth limp, 2s. 6d.

Doran. — Memories of our Great Towns; with Anecdotic Gleanings concerning their Worthies and their Oddities. By Dr. JOHN DORAN, F.S.A. With 38 Illustrations. New and Cheaper Edition, crown 8vo, cloth extra, 7s. 6d.

Drama, A Dictionary of the. Being a comprehensive Guide to the Plays, Playwrights, Players, and Playhouses of the United Kingdom and America, from the Earliest to the Present Times. By W. DAVENPORT ADAMS. (Uniform with BREWER'S "Reader's Handbook.") Crown 8vo, half-bound, 12s. 6d. [*In preparation.*

Dramatists, The Old. Crown 8vo, cloth extra, with Vignette Portraits, 6s. per Vol.

Ben Jonson's Works. With Notes Critical and Explanatory, and a Biographical Memoir by WM. GIFFORD. Edited by Colonel CUNNINGHAM. Three Vols.

Chapman's Works. Complete in Three Vols. Vol. I. contains the Plays complete, including the doubtful ones; Vol. II., the Poems and Minor Translations, with an Introductory Essay by ALGERNON CHAS. SWINBURNE; Vol. III., the Translations of the Iliad and Odyssey.

Marlowe's Works. Including his Translations. Edited, with Notes and Introduction, by Col. CUNNINGHAM. One Vol.

Massinger's Plays. From the Text of WILLIAM GIFFORD. Edited by Col. CUNNINGHAM. One Vol.

Dyer. — The Folk-Lore of Plants. By T. F. THISELTON DYER, M.A. Crown 8vo, cloth extra, 6s. [*In preparation.*

Edwards, Betham-. — Felicia: A Novel. By M. BETHAM-EDWARDS. Post 8vo, illustrated boards, 2s.; crown 8vo, cloth extra, 3s. 6d.

Early English Poets. Edited, with Introductions and Annotations, by Rev. A. B. GROSART, D.D. Crown 8vo, cloth boards, 6s. per Volume.

Fletcher's (Giles, B.D.) Complete Poems. One Vol.

Davies' (Sir John) Complete Poetical Works. Two Vols.

Herrick's (Robert) Complete Collected Poems. Three Vols.

Sidney's (Sir Philip) Complete Poetical Works. Three Vols.

Edwardes (Mrs. Annie), Novels by:

A Point of Honour. Post 8vo, illustrated boards, 2s.

Archie Lovell. Post 8vo, illustrated boards, 2s.; crown 8vo, cloth extra, 3s. 6d.

Eggleston. — Roxy: A Novel. By EDWARD EGGLESTON. Post 8vo, illustrated boards, 2s.; crown 8vo, cloth extra, 3s. 6d.

Emanuel. — On Diamonds and Precious Stones: their History, Value, and Properties; with Simple Tests for ascertaining their Reality. By HARRY EMANUEL, F.R.G.S. With numerous Illustrations, tinted and plain. Crown 8vo, cloth extra, gilt, 6s.

Englishman's House, The: A Practical Guide to all interested in Selecting or Building a House, with full Estimates of Cost, Quantities, &c. By C. J. RICHARDSON. Third Edition. With nearly 600 Illustrations. Crown 8vo, cloth extra, 7s. 6d.

Ewald (Alex. Charles, F.S.A.), Works by:

Stories from the State Papers. With an Autotype Facsimile. Crown 8vo, cloth extra, 6s.

The Life and Times of Prince Charles Stuart, Count of Albany, commonly called the Young Pretender. From the State Papers and other Sources. New and Cheaper Edition, with a Portrait, crown 8vo, cloth extra, 7s. 6d.

Fairholt. — Tobacco: Its History and Associations; with an Account of the Plant and its Manufacture, and its Modes of Use in all Ages and Countries. By F. W. FAIRHOLT, F.S.A. With Coloured Frontispiece and upwards of 100 Illustrations by the Author. Crown 8vo, cloth extra, 6s.

Familiar Allusions: A Handbook of Miscellaneous Information; including the Names of Celebrated Statues, Paintings, Palaces, Country Seats, Ruins, Churches, Ships, Streets, Clubs, Natural Curiosities, and the like. By WILLIAM A. WHEELER, Author of "Noted Names of Fiction;" and CHARLES G. WHEELER. Demy 8vo, cloth extra, 7s. 6d.

Faraday (Michael), Works by:

The Chemical History of a Candle: Lectures delivered before a Juvenile Audience at the Royal Institution. Edited by WILLIAM CROOKES, F.C.S. Post 8vo, cloth extra, with numerous Illustrations, 4s 6d.

On the Various Forces of Nature, and their Relations to each other: Lectures delivered before a Juvenile Audience at the Royal Institution. Edited by WILLIAM CROOKES, F.C.S. Post 8vo, cloth extra, with numerous Illustrations, 4s. 6d.

Fin-Bec.—The Cupboard
Papers: Observations on the Art of Living and Dining. By FIN-BEC. Post 8vo, cloth limp, 2s. 6d.

Fitzgerald (Percy), Works by:

The Recreations of a Literary Man; or, Does Writing Pay? With Recollections of some Literary Men, and a View of a Literary Man's Working Life. Crown 8vo, cloth extra, 6s.

The World Behind the Scenes. Crown 8vo, cloth extra, 3s. 6d.

Post 8vo, illustrated boards, 2s. each.
Bella Donna.
Never Forgotten.
The Second Mrs. Tillotson.
Polly.
Seventy-five Brooke Street.

Fletcher's (Giles, B.D.) Complete Poems: Christ's Victorie in Heaven, Christ's Victorie on Earth, Christ's Triumph over Death, and Minor Poems. With Memorial-Introduction and Notes, by the Rev. A. B. GROSART, D.D. Crown 8vo, cloth boards, 6s.

Fonblanque.—Filthy Lucre: A Novel. By ALBANY DE FONBLANQUE. Post 8vo, illustrated boards, 2s.

Francillon (R. E.), Novels by:
Crown 8vo, cloth extra, 3s. 6d. each; post 8vo, illust. boards, 2s. each.
Olympia.
Queen Cophetua.
One by One.
Esther's Glove. Fcap. 8vo, picture cover, 1s.

Frost (Thomas), Works by:
Crown 8vo, cloth extra, 3s. 6d. each.
Circus Life and Circus Celebrities.
The Lives of the Conjurers.
The Old Showmen and the Old London Fairs.

French Literature, History of.
By HENRI VAN LAUN. Complete in Three Vols., demy 8vo, cl. bds., 22s. 6d.

Gardening Books:

A Year's Work in Garden and Greenhouse: Practical Advice to Amateur Gardeners as to the Management of the Flower, Fruit, and Frame Garden. By GEORGE GLENNY. Post 8vo, cloth limp, 2s. 6d.

Our Kitchen Garden: The Plants we Grow, and How we Cook Them. By TOM JERROLD, Author of "The Garden that Paid the Rent," &c. Post 8vo, cloth limp, 2s. 6d.

Household Horticulture: A Gossip about Flowers. By TOM and JANE JERROLD. Illustrated. Post 8vo, cloth limp, 2s. 6d.

The Garden that Paid the Rent. By TOM JERROLD. Fcap. 8vo, illustrated cover, 1s; cloth limp, 1s. 6d.

My Garden Wild, and What I Grew there. By FRANCIS GEORGE HEATH. Crown 8vo, cloth extra, 5s.; gilt edges, 6s.

Garrett.—The Capel Girls: A Novel. By EDWARD GARRETT. Post 8vo, illustrated boards, 2s.; crown 8vo, cloth extra, 3s. 6d.

Gentleman's Magazine (The) for 1883. One Shilling Monthly. "The New Abelard," ROBERT BUCHANAN'S New Serial Story, was begun in the JANUARY Number of THE GENTLEMAN'S MAGAZINE. This Number contained many other interesting Articles, the continuation of JULIAN HAWTHORNE'S Story, "Dust," and a further instalment of "Science Notes," by W. MATTIEU WILLIAMS, F.R.A.S.

. *Now ready, the Volume for* JULY *to* DECEMBER, 1882, *cloth extra, price* 8s. 6d; *Cases for binding,* 2s. *each.*

German Popular Stories. Collected by the Brothers GRIMM, and Translated by EDGAR TAYLOR. Edited, with an Introduction, by JOHN RUSKIN. With 22 Illustrations on Steel by GEORGE CRUIKSHANK. Square 8vo, cloth extra, **6s. 6d.**; gilt edges, **7s. 6d.**

Gibbon (Charles), Novels by :

Each in crown 8vo, cloth extra, **3s. 6d.**; or post 8vo, illustrated boards, **2s.**

Robin Gray.
For Lack of Gold.
What will the World Say?
In Honour Bound.
In Love and War.
For the King.
Queen of the Meadow.
In Pastures Green.

Post 8vo, illustrated boards, **2s.**
The Dead Heart.

Crown 8vo, cloth extra, **3s. 6d.** each.
The Braes of Yarrow.
The Flower of the Forest.
A Heart's Problem.

Three Vols., crown 8vo, **31s. 6d.** each.
The Golden Shaft.
Of High Degree.

Fancy-Free. Two vols., crown 8vo.
[*In the press.*]

Gilbert (William), Novels by :

Post 8vo, illustrated boards, **2s.** each.
Dr. Austin's Guests.
The Wizard of the Mountain.
James Duke, Costermonger.

Gilbert (W. S.), Original Plays by: In Two Series, each complete in itself, price **2s. 6d.** each. FIRST SERIES contains The Wicked World—Pygmalion and Galatea—Charity—The Princess—The Palace of Truth—Trial by Jury. The SECOND SERIES contains Broken Hearts—Engaged—Sweethearts—Gretchen—Dan'l Druce—Tom Cobb—H.M.S. Pinafore—The Sorcerer—The Pirates of Penzance.

Glenny.—A Year's Work in Garden and Greenhouse: Practical Advice to Amateur Gardeners as to the Management of the Flower, Fruit, and Frame Garden. By GEORGE GLENNY. Post 8vo, cloth limp, **2s. 6d.**

Godwin.— Lives of the Necro. mancers. By WILLIAM GODWIN. Post 8vo, cloth limp, **2s.**

Golden Library, The :

Square 16mo (Tauchnitz size), cloth limp, **2s.** per volume.

Ballad History of England. By W. C. BENNETT.

Bayard Taylor's Diversions of the Echo Club.

Byron's Don Juan.

Godwin's (William) Lives of the Necromancers.

Holmes's Autocrat of the Breakfast Table. With an Introduction by G. A. SALA.

Holmes's Professor at the Breakfast Table.

Hood's Whims and Oddities. Complete. With all the original Illustrations.

Irving's (Washington) Tales of a Traveller.

Irving's (Washington) Tales of the Alhambra.

Jesse's (Edward) Scenes and Occupations of a Country Life.

Lamb's Essays of Elia. Both Series Complete in One Vol.

Leigh Hunt's Essays : A Tale for a Chimney Corner, and other Pieces. With Portrait, and Introduction by EDMUND OLLIER.

Mallory's (Sir Thomas) Mort d'Arthur : The Stories of King Arthur and of the Knights of the Round Table. Edited by B. MONTGOMERIE RANKING.

Pascal's Provincial Letters. A New Translation, with Historical Introduction and Notes, by T. M'CRIE, D.D.

Pope's Poetical Works. Complete.

Rochefoucauld's Maxims and Moral Reflections. With Notes, and Introductory Essay by SAINTE-BEUVE.

St. Pierre's Paul and Virginia, and The Indian Cottage. Edited, with Life, by the Rev. E. CLARKE.

Shelley's Early Poems, and Queen Mab. With Essay by LEIGH HUNT.

Shelley's Later Poems: Laon and Cythna, &c.

Shelley's Posthumous Poems, the Shelley Papers, &c.

Shelley's Prose Works, including A Refutation of Deism, Zastrozzi, St. Irvyne, &c.

White's Natural History of Selborne. Edited, with Additions, by THOMAS BROWN, F.L.S.

Golden Treasury of Thought,
The: An ENCYCLOPÆDIA OF QUOTA-
TIONS from Writers of all Times and
Countries. Selected and Edited by
THEODORE TAYLOR. Crown 8vo, cloth
gilt and gilt edges, 7s. 6d.

Gordon Cumming. — In the
Hebrides. By C. F. GORDON CUMMING,
Author of "At Home in Fiji." With
Autotype Facsimile and numerous
full-page Illustrations. Demy 8vo,
cloth extra, 8s. 6d. [*In preparation.*

Graham. — The Professor's
Wife: A Story. By LEONARD GRAHAM.
Fcap. 8vo, picture cover, 1s.; cloth
extra, 2s. 6d.

Greeks and Romans, The Life
of the, Described from Antique Monu-
ments. By ERNST GUHL and W.
KONER. Translated from the Third
German Edition, and Edited by Dr.
F. HUEFFER. With 545 Illustrations.
New and Cheaper Edition, demy 8vo,
cloth extra, 7s. 6d.

Greenwood (James),Works by :
The Wilds of London. Crown 8vo,
cloth extra, 3s. 6d.
Low-Life Deeps: An Account of the
Strange Fish to be Found There.
Crown 8vo, cloth extra, 3s. 6d.
Dick Temple: A Novel. Post 8vo,
illustrated boards, 2s.

Guyot. — The Earth and Man :
or, Physical Geography in its relation
to the History of Mankind. By
ARNOLD GUYOT. With Additions by
Professors AGASSIZ, PIERCE, and GRAY:
12 Maps and Engravings on Steel,
some Coloured, and copious Index.
Crown 8vo, cloth extra, gilt, 4s. 6d.

Hair (The): Its Treatment in
Health, Weakness, and Disease.
Translated from the German of Dr. J.
PINCUS. Crown 8vo, 1s.; cloth, 1s. 6d.

Hake (Dr. Thomas Gordon).
Poems by :
Maiden Ecstasy. Small 4to, cloth
extra, 8s.
New Symbols. Crown 8vo, cloth
extra, 6s.
Legends of the Morrow. Crown 8vo,
cloth extra, 6s.
The Serpent Play. Crown 8vo, cloth
extra, 6s.

Half-Hours with Foreign Nov-
elists. With Notices of their Lives
and Writings. By HELEN and ALICE
ZIMMERN. A New Edition. Two Vols.,
crown 8vo, cloth extra, 12s.

Hall.—Sketches of Irish Cha-
racter. By Mrs. S. C. HALL. With
numerous Illustrations on Steel and
Wood by MACLISE, GILBERT, HARVEY,
and G. CRUIKSHANK. Medium 8vo,
cloth extra, gilt, 7s. 6d.

Halliday.—Every-day Papers.
By ANDREW HALLIDAY. Post 8vo,
illustrated boards, 2s.

Handwriting, The Philosophy
of. With over 100 Facsimiles and Explanatory Text. By DON FELIX DE
SALAMANCA. Post 8vo, cloth limp, 2s. 6d.

Hanky-Panky : A Collection of
Very Easy Tricks, Very Difficult Tricks,
White Magic, Sleight of Hand, &c.
Edited by W. H. CREMER. With 200
Illustrations. Crown 8vo, cloth extra,
4s. 6d.

Hardy (Lady Duffus). — Paul
Wynter's Sacrifice: A Story. By
Lady DUFFUS HARDY. Post 8vo, illust-
boards, 2s.

Hardy (Thomas).—Under the
Greenwood Tree. By THOMAS HARDY,
Author of "Far from the Madding
Crowd." Crown 8vo, cloth extra,
3s. 6d. ; post 8vo, illustrated boards, 2s.

Haweis (Mrs. H. R.), Works by :
The Art of Dress. With numerous
Illustrations. Small 8vo, illustrated
cover, 1s.; cloth limp, 1s. 6d.
The Art of Beauty. Square 8vo,
cloth extra, gilt edges, with Co-
loured Frontispiece and nearly 100
Illustrations, 10s. 6d.
The Art of Decoration. Square 8vo,
handsomely bound and profusely
Illustrated, 10s. 6d.
Chaucer for Children : A Golden
Key. With Eight Coloured Pictures
and numerous Woodcuts. New
Edition, small 4to, cloth extra, 6s.
Chaucer for Schools. Demy 8vo,
cloth limp, 2s. 6d.

Haweis (Rev. H. R.).—American
Humorists. Including WASHINGTON
IRVING, OLIVER WENDELL HOLMES,
JAMES RUSSELL LOWELL, ARTEMUS
WARD, MARK TWAIN, and BRET HARTE.
By the Rev. H. R. HAWEIS, M.A.
Crown 8vo, cloth extra, 6s.

Hawthorne (Julian), Novels by.
Crown 8vo, cloth extra, 3s. 6d. each;
post 8vo, illustrated boards, 2s. each.

> **Garth.**
> **Ellice Quentin.**
> **Sebastian Strome.**

Mrs. Gainsborough's Diamonds.
Fcap. 8vo, illustrated cover, 1s.;
cloth extra, 2s. 6d.

Prince Saroni's Wife, &c. Crown 8vo,
cloth extra, 3s. 6d.

Dust: A Novel. Three Vols., crown
8vo, 31s. 6d.

Heath (F. G.). — My Garden
Wild, and What I Grew There. By
FRANCIS GEORGE HEATH, Author of
"The Fern World," &c. Crown 8vo,
cloth extra, 5s.; cloth gilt, and gilt
edges, 6s.

Helps (Sir Arthur), Works by :
Animals and their Masters. Post
8vo, cloth limp, 2s. 6d.

Ivan de Biron: A Novel. Crown 8vo,
cloth extra, 3s. 6d.; post 8vo, illustrated boards, 2s.

Heptalogia (The); or, The
Seven against Sense. A Cap with
Seven Bells. Crown 8vo, cloth extra,
6s.

Herbert.—The Poems of Lord
Herbert of Cherbury. Edited, with
an Introduction, by J. CHURTON
COLLINS. Crown 8vo, bound in parchment, 8s.; Large-Paper copies (only
50 printed), 15s.

Herrick's (Robert) Hesperides,
Noble Numbers, and Complete Collected Poems. With Memorial-Introduction and Notes by the Rev. A. B.
GROSART, D.D., Steel Portrait, Index
of First Lines, and Glossarial Index,
&c. Three Vols., crown 8vo, cloth
boards, 18s.

Hesse-Wartegg (Chevalier
Ernst von), Works by :
Tunis: The Land and the People.
With 22 Illustrations. Crown 8vo,
cloth extra, 3s. 6d.

The New South West: Travelling
Sketches from Kansas, New Mexico,
Arizona, and Northern Mexico.
With 100 fine Illustrations and 3
Maps. Demy 8vo, cloth extra,
14s.　　　　　*[In preparation.*

Hindley (Charles), Works by :
Crown 8vo, cloth extra, 3s. 6d. each.

Tavern Anecdotes and Sayings : In-
cluding the Origin of Signs, and
Reminiscences connected with
Taverns, Coffee Houses, Clubs, &c.
With Illustrations.

The Life and Adventures of a Cheap
Jack. By One of the Fraternity.
Edited by CHARLES HINDLEY.

Holmes (Oliver Wendell), Works
by :
The Autocrat of the Breakfast-
Table. Illustrated by J. GORDON
THOMSON. Post 8vo, cloth limp,
2s. 6d.; another Edition in smaller
type, with an Introduction by G. A.
SALA. Post 8vo, cloth limp, 2s.

The Professor at the Breakfast-
Table; with the Story of Iris. Post
8vo, cloth limp, 2s.

Holmes. — The Science of
Voice Production and Voice Preser-
vation: A Popular Manual for the
Use of Speakers and Singers. By
GORDON HOLMES, M.D. Crown 8vo,
cloth limp, with Illustrations, 2s. 6d.

Hood (Thomas):
Hood's Choice Works, in Prose and
Verse. Including the Cream of the
Comic Annuals. With Life of the
Author, Portrait, and 200 Illustra-
tions. Crown 8vo, cloth extra, 7s. 6d.

Hood's Whims and Oddities. Complete. With all the original Illustrations. Post 8vo, cloth limp, 2s.

Hood (Tom), Works by :
From Nowhere to the North Pole:
A Noah's Arkæological Narrative.
With 25 Illustrations by W. BRUN-
TON and E. C. BARNES. Square
crown 8vo, cloth extra, gilt edges, 6s.

A Golden Heart. A Novel. Post 8vo,
illustrated boards, 2s.

Hook's (Theodore) Choice Hu-
morous Works, including his Ludi-
crous Adventures, Bons Mots, Puns and
Hoaxes. With a New Life of the
Author, Portraits, Facsimiles, and
Illustrations. Crown 8vo, cloth extra,
gilt, 7s. 6d.

Horne.—Orion : An Epic Poem,
in Three Books. By RICHARD HEN-
GIST HORNE. With Photographic
Portrait from a Medallion by SUM-
MERS. Tenth Edition, crown 8vo,
cloth extra, 7s.

Howell.—Conflicts of Capital and Labour. Historically and Economically considered: Being a History and Review of the Trade Unions of Great Britain, showing their Origin, Progress, Constitution, and Objects, in their Political, Social, Economical, and Industrial Aspects. By GEORGE HOWELL. Crown 8vo, cloth extra, 7s. 6d.

Hueffer.—The Troubadours: A History of Provencal Life and Literature in the Middle Ages. By FRANCIS HUEFFER. Demy 8vo, cloth extra, 12s. 6d.

Hugo. — The Hunchback of Notre Dame. By VICTOR HUGO. Post 8vo, illustrated boards, 2s.

Hunt.—Essays by Leigh Hunt. A Tale for a Chimney Corner, and other Pieces. With Portrait and Introduction by EDMUND OLLIER. Post 8vo, cloth limp, 2s.

Hunt (Mrs. Alfred), Novels by:
Thornicroft's Model. Crown 8vo, cloth extra, 3s. 6d.; post 8vo, illustrated boards, 2s.
The Leaden Casket. Crown 8vo, cloth extra, 3s 6d.; post 8vo, illustrated boards, 2s.
Self Condemned. Three Vols., crown 8vo, 31s. 6d.

Ingelow.—Fated to be Free: A Novel. By JEAN INGELOW. Crown 8vo, cloth extra, 3s. 6d.; post 8vo, illustrated boards, 2s.

Ireland under the Land Act: Letters to the *Standard* during the Crisis. Containing the most recent Information about the State of the Country, the Popular Leaders, the League, the Working of the Sub-Commissions, &c. With Leading Cases under the Act, giving the Evidence in full; Judicial Dicta, &c. By E. CANTWALL. Crown 8vo, cloth extra, 6s.

Irving (Washington), Works by:
Post 8vo, cloth limp, 2s. each.
Tales of a Traveller.
Tales of the Alhambra.

James.—Confidence: A Novel. By HENRY JAMES, Jun. Crown 8vo, cloth extra, 3s. 6d.; post 8vo, illustrated boards, 2s.

Janvier.—Practical Keramics for Students. By CATHERINE A. JANVIER. Crown 8vo, cloth extra, 6s.

Jay (Harriett), Novels by. Each crown 8vo, cloth extra, 3s. 6d.; or post 8vo, illustrated boards, 2s.
The Dark Colleen.
The Queen of Connaught.

Jefferies.—Nature near London. By RICHARD JEFFERIES, Author of "The Gamekeeper at Home." Crown 8vo, cloth extra, 6s.

Jennings (H. J.).—Curiosities of Criticism. By HENRY J. JENNINGS. Post 8vo, cloth limp, 2s. 6d.

Jennings (Hargrave). — The Rosicrucians: Their Rites and Mysteries. With Chapters on the Ancient Fire and Serpent Worshippers. By HARGRAVE JENNINGS. With Five full-page Plates and upwards of 300 Illustrations. A New Edition, crown 8vo, cloth extra, 7s. 6d.

Jerrold (Tom), Works by:
The Garden that Paid the Rent. By TOM JERROLD. Feap. 8vo, illustrated cover, 1s.; cloth limp, 1s. 6d.
Household Horticulture: A Gossip about Flowers. By TOM and JANE JERROLD. Illustrated. Post 8vo, cloth limp, 2s. 6d.
Our Kitchen Garden: The Plants we Grow, and How we Cook Them. By TOM JERROLD. Post 8vo, cloth limp, 2s 6d.

Jesse.—Scenes and Occupations of a Country Life. By EDWARD JESSE. Post 8vo cloth limp, 2s.

Jones (William, F.S.A.), Works by:
Finger Ring Lore: Historical, Legendary, and Anecdotal. With over 200 Illustrations. Crown 8vo, cloth extra, 7s. 6d.
Credulities, Past and Present; including the Sea and Seamen, Miners, Talismans, Word and Letter Divination, Exorcising and Blessing of Animals, Birds, Eggs, Luck, &c. With an Etched Frontispiece. Crown 8vo, cloth extra, 7s. 6d.
Crowns and Coronations: A History of Regalia in all Times and Countries. With about 100 Illustrations, many full-page. Crown 8vo, cloth extra, 7s. 6d. [*In preparation.*

Jonson's (Ben) Works. With Notes Critical and Explanatory, and a Biographical Memoir by WILLIAM GIFFORD. Edited by Colonel CUNNINGHAM. Three Vols., crown 8vo, cloth extra, 18s.; or separately, 6s. per Volume.

Josephus, The Complete Works of. Translated by WHISTON. Containing both "The Antiquities of the Jews" and "The Wars of the Jews." Two Vols., 8vo, with 52 Illustrations and Maps, cloth extra, gilt, 14s.

Kavanagh.—The Pearl Fountain, and other Fairy Stories. By BRIDGET and JULIA KAVANAGH. With Thirty Illustrations by J. MOYR SMITH. Small 8vo, cloth gilt, 6s.

Kempt.—Pencil and Palette: Chapters on Art and Artists. By ROBERT KEMPT. Post 8vo, cloth limp, 2s. 6d.

Kingsley (Henry), Novels by: Each crown 8vo, cloth extra, 3s. 6d.; or post 8vo, illustrated boards, 2s.

    Oakshott Castle.
    Number Seventeen.

Lace (Old Point), and How to Copy and Imitate it. By DAISY WATERHOUSE HAWKINS. With 17 Illustrations by the Author. Crown 8vo, illustrated boards, 2s. 6d.

Lamb (Charles):

Mary and Charles Lamb: Their Poems, Letters, and Remains. With Reminiscences and Notes by W. CAREW HAZLITT. With Hancock's Portrait of the Essayist, Facsimiles of the Title-pages of the rare First Editions of Lamb's and Coleridge's Works, and numerous Illustrations. Crown 8vo, cloth extra, 10s. 6d.

Lamb's Complete Works, in Prose and Verse, reprinted from the Original Editions, with many Pieces hitherto unpublished. Edited, with Notes and Introduction, by R. H. SHEPHERD. With Two Portraits and Facsimile of a Page of the "Essay on Roast Pig." Crown 8vo, cloth extra, 7s. 6d.

The Essays of Elia. Complete Edition. Post 8vo, cloth extra, 2s.

Poetry for Children, and Prince Dorus. By CHARLES LAMB. Carefully Reprinted from unique copies. Small 8vo, cloth extra, 5s.

Lane's Arabian Nights, &c.:

The Thousand and One Nights: commonly called, in England, "THE ARABIAN NIGHTS' ENTERTAINMENTS." A New Translation from the Arabic, with copious Notes, by EDWARD WILLIAM LANE. Illustrated by many hundred Engravings on Wood, from Original Designs by WM. HARVEY. A New Edition, from a Copy annotated by the Translator, edited by his Nephew, EDWARD STANLEY POOLE. With a Preface by STANLEY LANE-POOLE. Three Vols., demy 8vo, cloth extra, 7s. 6d. each.

Arabian Society in the Middle Ages: Studies from "The Thousand and One Nights." By EDWARD WM. LANE, Author of "The Modern Egyptians," &c. Edited by STANLEY LANE-POOLE. Cr. 8vo, cloth extra, 6s.

Lares and Penates; or, The Background of Life. By FLORENCE CADDY. Crown 8vo, cloth extra, 6s.

Larwood (Jacob), Works by:

The Story of the London Parks. With Illustrations. Crown 8vo, cloth extra, 3s. 6d.

Clerical Anecdotes. Post 8vo, cloth limp, 2s. 6d.

Forensic Anecdotes. Post 8vo, cloth limp, 2s. 6d.

Theatrical Anecdotes. Post 8vo, cloth limp, 2s. 6d.

Leigh (Henry S.), Works by:

Carols of Cockayne. With numerous Illustrations. Post 8vo, cloth limp, 2s. 6d.

A Town Garland. Crown 8vo, cloth extra, 6s.

Jeux d'Esprit. Collected and Edited by HENRY S. LEIGH. Post 8vo, cloth limp, 2s. 6d.

Linton (E. Lynn), Works by:

Witch Stories. Post 8vo, cloth limp, 2s. 6d.

The True Story of Joshua Davidson. Post 8vo, cloth limp, 2s. 6d.

Crown 8vo, cloth extra, 3s. 6d. each; post 8vo, illustrated boards, 2s.

    Patricia Kemball.
    The Atonement of Leam Dundas.
    The World Well Lost.
    Under which Lord?
    With a Silken Thread.
    The Rebel of the Family.
    "My Love!"

Life in London; or, The History of Jerry Hawthorn and Corinthian Tom. With the whole of CRUIK-SHANK'S Illustrations, in Colours, after the Originals. Crown 8vo, cloth extra, 7s. 6d.

Longfellow :

Longfellow's Complete Prose Works. Including "Outre Mer," "Hyperion," "Kavanagh," "The Poets and Poetry of Europe," and "Driftwood." With Portrait and Illustrations by VALENTINE BROMLEY. Crown 8vo, cloth extra, 7s. 6d.

Longfellow's Poetical Works. Carefully Reprinted from the Original Editions. With numerous fine Illustrations on Steel and Wood. Crown 8vo, cloth extra, 7s. 6d.

Lucy.—Gideon Fleyce: A Novel. By HENRY W. LUCY. Three Vols., crown 8vo, 31s. 6d.

Lunatic Asylum, My Experiences in a. By A SANE PATIENT. Crown 8vo, cloth extra, 5s.

Lusiad (The) of Camoens. Translated into English Spenserian Verse by ROBERT FRENCH DUFF. Demy 8vo, with Fourteen full-page Plates, cloth boards, 18s.

McCarthy (Justin, M.P.),Works by :

A History of Our Own Times, from the Accession of Queen Victoria to the General Election of 1880. Four Vols. demy 8vo, cloth extra, 12s. each.—Also a POPULAR EDITION, in Four Vols. crown 8vo, cloth extra, 6s. each.

A Short History of Our Own Times. One Volume, crown 8vo, cloth extra, 6s. [*In preparation.*]

History of the Four Georges. Four Vols. demy 8vo, cloth extra, 12s. each. [*In preparation.*]

Crown 8vo, cloth extra, 3s. 6d. each ; post 8vo, illustrated boards, 2s. each.

Dear Lady Disdain.
The Waterdale Neighbours.
My Enemy's Daughter.
A Fair Saxon.
Linley Rochford.
Miss Misanthrope.
Donna Quixote.

The Comet of a Season. Crown 8vo, cloth extra, 3s. 6d.

McCarthy (Justin H.), Works by :

An Outline of the History of Ireland, from the Earliest Times to the Present Day. Crown 8vo, 1s. ; cloth, 1s. 6d.

Serapion, and other Poems. Crown 8vo, cloth extra, 6s.

MacDonald (George, LL.D.), Works by :

The Princess and Curdie. With 11 Illustrations by JAMES ALLEN. Small crown 8vo, cloth extra, 5s.

Gutta-Percha Willie, the Working Genius. With 9 Illustrations by ARTHUR HUGHES. Square 8vo, cloth extra, 3s. 6d.

Paul Faber, Surgeon. With a Frontispiece by J. E. MILLAIS. Crown 8vo, cloth extra, 3s. 6d. ; post 8vo, illustrated boards, 2s.

Thomas Wingfold, Curate. With a Frontispiece by C. J. STANILAND. Crown 8vo, cloth extra, 3s. 6d. ; post 8vo, illustrated boards, 2s.

Macdonell.—Quaker Cousins: A Novel. By AGNES MACDONELL. Crown 8vo, cloth extra, 3s. 6d.; post 8vo, illustrated boards, 2s.

Macgregor. — Pastimes and Players. Notes on Popular Games. By ROBERT MACGREGOR. Post 8vo, cloth limp, 2s. 6d.

Macquoid (Mrs.), Works by :

In the Ardennes. With 50 fine Illustrations by THOMAS R. MACQUOID. Square 8vo, cloth extra, 10s. 6d.

Pictures and Legends from Normandy and Brittany. With numerous Illustrations by THOMAS R. MACQUOID. Square 8vo, cloth gilt, 10s. 6d.

Through Normandy. With 90 Illustrations by T. R. MACQUOID. Square 8vo, cloth extra, 7s. 6d.

Through Brittany. With numerous Illustrations by T. R. MACQUOID. Square 8vo, cloth extra, 7s. 6d.

About Yorkshire. With about 70 Illustrations by T. R. MACQUOID, Engraved by SWAIN. Square 8vo, cloth extra, 10s. 6d.

The Evil Eye, and other Stories. Crown 8vo, cloth extra, 3s. 6d.; post 8vo, illustrated boards, 2s.

Lost Rose, and other Stories. Crown 8vo, cloth extra, 3s. 6d ; post 8vo, illustrated boards, 2s.

Maclise Portrait-Gallery (The)

of Illustrious Literary Characters; with Memoirs—Biographical, Critical, Bibliographical, and Anecdotal—illustrative of the Literature of the former half of the Present Century. By WILLIAM BATES, B.A. With 85 Portraits printed on an India Tint. Crown 8vo, cloth extra, 7s. 6d. [*In the press.*

Magician's Own Book (The):

Performances with Cups and Balls, Eggs, Hats, Handkerchiefs, &c. All from actual Experience. Edited by W. H. CREMER. With 200 Illustrations. Crown 8vo, cloth extra, 4s. 6d.

Magic No Mystery: Tricks with

Cards, Dice, Balls, &c., with fully descriptive Directions; the Art of Secret Writing; Training of Performing Animals, &c. With Coloured Frontispiece and many Illustrations. Crown 8vo, cloth extra, 4s. 6d.

Magna Charta. An exact Fac-

simile of the Original in the British Museum, printed on fine plate paper, 3 feet by 2 feet, with Arms and Seals emblazoned in Gold and Colours. Price 5s.

Mallock (W. H.), Works by:

The New Republic; or, Culture, Faith and Philosophy in an English Country House. Post 8vo, cloth limp, 2s. 6d.; Cheap Edition, illustrated boards, 2s.

The New Paul and Virginia; or, Positivism on an Island. Post 8vo, cloth limp, 2s. 6d.

Poems. Small 4to, bound in parchment, 8s.

Is Life worth Living? Crown 8vo, cloth extra, 6s.

A Romance of the Nineteenth Century. Second Edition, with a Preface. Two Vols., crown 8vo, 21s.

Mallory's (Sir Thomas) Mort

d'Arthur: The Stories of King Arthur and of the Knights of the Round Table. Edited by B. MONTGOMERIE RANKING. Post 8vo, cloth limp, 2s.

Marryat (Florence). Novels by:

Crown 8vo, cloth extra, 3s. 6d. each; or post 8vo, illustrated boards, 2s.

Open! Sesame!
Written in Fire.

Post 8vo, illustrated boards, 2s each.

A Harvest of Wild Oats.
A Little Stepson.
Fighting the Air.

Marlowe's Works. Including

his Translations. Edited, with Notes and Introduction, by Col. CUNNINGHAM. Crown 8vo, cloth extra, 6s.

Mark Twain, Works by:

The Choice Works of Mark Twain. Revised and Corrected throughout by the Author. With Life, Portrait, and numerous Illustrations. Crown 8vo, cloth extra, 7s. 6d.

The Adventures of Tom Sawyer. With 100 Illustrations. Small 8vo, cloth extra, 7s. 6d. CHEAP EDITION, illustrated boards, 2s.

An Idle Excursion, and other Sketches. Post 8vo, illustrated boards, 2s.

The Prince and the Pauper. With nearly 200 Illustrations. Crown 8vo, cloth extra, 7s. 6d.

The Innocents Abroad; or, The New Pilgrim's Progress: Being some Account of the Steamship "Quaker City's" Pleasure Excursion to Europe and the Holy Land. With 234 Illustrations. Crown 8vo, cloth extra, 7s. 6d. CHEAP EDITION (under the title of "MARK TWAIN'S PLEASURE TRIP"), post 8vo, illust. boards, 2s.

A Tramp Abroad. With 314 Illustrations. Crown 8vo, cloth extra, 7s. 6d.

The Stolen White Elephant, &c Crown 8vo, cloth extra, 6s.

Life on the Mississippi. With about 300 Original Illustrations. Crown 8vo, cloth extra, 7s. 6d.

Massinger's Plays. From the

Text of WILLIAM GIFFORD. Edited by Col. CUNNINGHAM. Crown 8vo, cloth extra, 6s.

Mayhew.—London Characters

and the Humorous Side of London Life. By HENRY MAYHEW. With numerous Illustrations. Crown 8vo, cloth extra, 3s. 6d.

Mayfair Library. The:

Post 8vo, cloth limp, 2s. 6d. per Volume.

A Journey Round My Room. By XAVIER DE MAISTRE. Translated by HENRY ATTWELL.

Latter-Day Lyrics. Edited by W. DAVENPORT ADAMS.

Quips and Quiddities. Selected by W. DAVENPORT ADAMS.

The Agony Column of "The Times," from 1800 to 1870. Edited, with an Introduction, by ALICE CLAY.

Balzac's "Comedie Humaine" and its Author. With Translations by H. H. WALKER.

MAYFAIR LIBRARY, continued—

Melancholy Anatomised: A Popular Abridgment of "Burton's Anatomy of Melancholy."

Gastronomy as a Fine Art. By BRILLAT-SAVARIN.

The Speeches of Charles Dickens.

Literary Frivolities, Fancies, Follies, and Frolics. By W. T. DOBSON.

Poetical Ingenuities and Eccentricities. Selected and Edited by W. T. DOBSON.

The Cupboard Papers. By FIN-BEC.

Original Plays by W. S. GILBERT. FIRST SERIES. Containing: The Wicked World — Pygmalion and Galatea — Charity — The Princess — The Palace of Truth — Trial by Jury.

Original Plays by W. S. GILBERT. SECOND SERIES. Containing: Broken Hearts — Engaged — Sweethearts — Gretchen — Dan'l Druce — Tom Cobb — H.M.S. Pinafore — The Sorcerer — The Pirates of Penzance.

Animals and their Masters. By Sir ARTHUR HELPS.

Curiosities of Criticism. By HENRY J. JENNINGS.

The Autocrat of the Breakfast Table. By OLIVER WENDELL HOLMES. Illustrated by J. GORDON THOMSON.

Pencil and Palette. By ROBERT KEMPT.

Clerical Anecdotes. By JACOB LARWOOD.

Forensic Anecdotes; or, Humour and Curiosities of the Law and Men of Law. By JACOB LARWOOD.

Theatrical Anecdotes. By JACOB LARWOOD.

Carols of Cockayne. By HENRY S. LEIGH.

Jeux d'Esprit. Edited by HENRY S. LEIGH.

True History of Joshua Davidson. By E. LYNN LINTON.

Witch Stories. By E. LYNN LINTON.

Pastimes and Players. By ROBERT MACGREGOR.

The New Paul and Virginia. By W. H. MALLOCK.

The New Republic. By W. H. MALLOCK.

Muses of Mayfair. Edited by H. CHOLMONDELEY-PENNELL.

Thoreau: His Life and Aims. By H. A. PAGE.

Puck on Pegasus. By H. CHOLMONDELEY-PENNELL.

Puniana. By the Hon. HUGH ROWLEY.

MAYFAIR LIBRARY, continued—

More Puniana. By the Hon. HUGH ROWLEY.

The Philosophy of Handwriting. By DON FELIX DE SALAMANCA.

By Stream and Sea. By WILLIAM SENIOR.

Old Stories Re-told. By WALTER THORNBURY.

Leaves from a Naturalist's Note Book. By Dr. ANDREW WILSON.

Merry Circle (The): A Book of

New Intellectual Games and Amusements. By CLARA BELLEW. With numerous Illustrations. Crown 8vo, cloth extra, 4s. 6d.

Middlemass (Jean), Novels by:

Touch and Go. Crown 8vo, cloth extra, 3s. 6d.; post 8vo, illustrated boards, 2s.

Mr. Dorillion. Post 8vo, illustrated boards, 2s.

Miller. — Physiology for the

Young; or, The House of Life: Human Physiology, with its application to the Preservation of Health. For use in Classes and Popular Reading. With numerous Illustrations. By Mrs. F. FENWICK MILLER. Small 8vo, cloth limp, 2s. 6d.

Milton (J. L.), Works by:

The Hygiene of the Skin. A Concise Set of Rules for the Management of the Skin; with Directions for Diet, Wines, Soaps, Baths, &c. Small 8vo, 1s.; cloth extra, 1s. 6d.

The Bath in Diseases of the Skin. Small 8vo, 1s.; cloth extra, 1s. 6d.

The Laws of Life, and their Relation to Diseases of the Skin. Small 8vo, 1s.; cloth extra, 1s. 6d.

Moncrieff. — The Abdication;

or, Time Tries All. An Historical Drama. By W. D. SCOTT-MONCRIEFF. With Seven Etchings by JOHN PETTIE, R.A., W. Q. ORCHARDSON, R.A., J. MACWHIRTER, A.R.A., COLIN HUNTER, R. MACBETH, and TOM GRAHAM. Large 4to, bound in buckram, 21s.

Murray (D. Christie), Novels by:

A Life's Atonement. Crown 8vo, cloth extra, 3s. 6d.; post 8vo, illustrated boards, 2s.

Joseph's Coat. With Illustrations by F. BARNARD. Crown 8vo, cloth extra, 3s. 6d.

D. C. MURRAY'S NOVELS, *continued*—

Coals of Fire. With Illustrations by ARTHUR HOPKINS and others. Crown 8vo, cloth extra, 3s. 6d.

A Model Father, and other Stories. Crown 8vo, cloth extra, 3s. 6d. ; post 8vo, illustrated boards, 2s.   [*July.*

Val Strange: A Story of the Primrose Way. Three Vols., crown 8vo, 31s.6d.

Hearts. Three Vols., crown 8vo, 31s. 6d.

By the Gate of the Sea. Two Vols., post 8vo, 12s.   [*Shortly.*

North Italian Folk. By Mrs. COMYNS CARR. Illustrated by RANDOLPH CALDECOTT. Square 8vo, cloth extra, 7s. 6d.

Number Nip (Stories about), the Spirit of the Giant Mountains. Retold for Children by WALTER GRAHAME. With Illustrations by J. MOYR SMITH. Post 8vo, cloth extra, 5s.

Oliphant. — Whiteladies: A Novel. With Illustrations by ARTHUR HOPKINS and HENRY WOODS. Crown 8vo, cloth extra, 3s. 6d. ; post 8vo, illustrated boards, 2s.

O Reilly.—Phœbe's Fortunes: A Novel. With Illustrations by HENRY TUCK. Post 8vo, illustrated boards, 2s.

O Shaughnessy (Arth.), Works by :

Songs of a Worker. Fcap. 8vo, cloth extra, 7s. 6d.

Music and Moonlight. Fcap. 8vo, cloth extra, 7s. 6d.

Lays of France. Crown 8vo, cloth extra, 10s. 6d.

Ouida, Novels by. Crown 8vo, cloth extra, 5s. each ; post 8vo, illustrated boards, 2s. each.

Held in Bondage.
Strathmore.
Chandos.
Under Two Flags.
Idalia.
Cecil Castlemaine's Gage.
Tricotrin.
Puck.
Folle Farine.
A Dog of Flanders.
Pascarel.
Two Little Wooden Shoes.

OUIDA'S NOVELS, *continued*—

Signa.
In a Winter City.
Ariadne.
Friendship.
Moths.
Pipistrello.
A Village Commune.

In Maremma. Crown 8vo, cloth extra, 5s.

Bimbi: Stories for Children. Square 8vo, cloth gilt, cinnamon edges, 7s.6d.

Wanda: A Novel. Three Vols., crown 8vo, 31s. 6d.

Wisdom, Poetry, and Pathos, Selected from the Works of OUIDA. By F. S. MORRIS. Small crown 8vo, cloth extra, 5s.   [*In the press.*

Page (H. A.), Works by :

Thoreau: His Life and Aims: A Study. With a Portrait. Post 8vo, cloth limp, 2s. 6d.

Lights on the Way: Some Tales within a Tale. By the late J. H. ALEXANDER, B.A. Edited by H. A. PAGE. Crown 8vo, cloth extra, 6s.

Pascal's Provincial Letters. A New Translation, with Historical Introduction and Notes, by T. M'CRIE, D.D. Post 8vo, cloth limp, 2s.

Paul Ferroll :

Post 8vo, illustrated boards, 2s. each.
Paul Ferroll : A Novel.
Why Paul Ferroll Killed His Wife.

Payn (James), Novels by :

Each crown 8vo, cloth extra, 3s. 6d. ; or post 8vo, illustrated boards, 2s.

Lost Sir Massingberd.
The Best of Husbands.
Walter's Word.
Halves.
Fallen Fortunes.
What He Cost Her.
Less Black than We're Painted
By Proxy.
Under One Roof.
High Spirits.
Carlyon's Year.
A Confidential Agent
Some Private Views.
From Exile.

JAMES PAYN'S NOVELS, *continued—*

Post 8vo, illustrated boards, 2s. each.

A Perfect Treasure.
Bentinck's Tutor.
Murphy's Master.
A County Family.
At Her Mercy.
A Woman's Vengeance.
Cecil's Tryst.
The Clyffards of Clyffe.
The Family Scapegrace.
The Foster Brothers.
Found Dead.
Gwendoline's Harvest.
Humorous Stories.
Like Father, Like Son.
A Marine Residence.
Married Beneath Him.
Mirk Abbey.
Not Wooed, but Won.
Two Hundred Pounds Reward.

A Grape from a Thorn. With Illustrations by W. SMALL. Crown 8vo, cloth extra, 3s. 6d.

For Cash Only. Crown 8vo, cloth extra, 3s. 6d.

Kit: A Memory. Three Vols., crown 8vo, 31s. 6d.

Pennell (H. Cholmondeley),
Works by: Post 8vo, cloth limp, 2s. 6d. each.

Puck on Pegasus. With Illustrations.
The Muses of Mayfair. Vers de Société, Selected and Edited by H. C. PENNELL.

Pirkis.—Trooping with Crows: A Story. By CATHERINE PIRKIS. Fcap. 8vo, picture cover, 1s.

Planche (J. R.), Works by:

The Encyclopædia of Costume; or, A Dictionary of Dress—Regal, Ecclesiastical, Civil, and Military—from the Earliest Period in England to the Reign of George the Third. Including Notices of Contemporaneous Fashions on the Continent, and a General History of the Costumes of the Principal Countries of Europe. Two Vols., demy 4to, half morocco, profusely Illustrated with Coloured and Plain Plates and Woodcuts, £7 7s. The Volumes may also be had *separately* (each complete in itself) at £3 13s. 6d. each: Vol. I. THE DICTIONARY. Vol. II. A GENERAL HISTORY OF COSTUME IN EUROPE.

PLANCHE'S WORKS, *continued—*

The Pursuivant of Arms; or, Heraldry Founded upon Facts. With Coloured Frontispiece and 200 Illustrations. Crown 8vo, cloth extra, 7s. 6d.

Songs and Poems, from 1819 to 1879. Edited, with an Introduction, by his Daughter, Mrs. MACKARNESS. Crown 8vo, cloth extra, 6s.

Play-time: Sayings and Doings of Babyland. By EDWARD STANFORD. Large 4to, handsomely printed in Colours, 4s. 6d. [*Shortly.*

Plutarch's Lives of Illustrious Men. Translated from the Greek, with Notes Critical and Historical, and a Life of Plutarch, by JOHN and WILLIAM LANGHORNE. Two Vols., 8vo, cloth extra, with Portraits, 10s. 6d.

Poe (Edgar Allan):—

The Choice Works, in Prose and Poetry, of EDGAR ALLAN POE. With an Introductory Essay by CHARLES BAUDELAIRE, Portrait and Facsimiles. Crown 8vo, cloth extra, 7s. 6d.

The Mystery of Marie Roget, and other Stories. Post 8vo, illustrated boards, 2s.

Pope's Poetical Works. Complete in One Volume. Post 8vo, cloth limp, 2s.

Price.—Valentina: A Sketch. By E. C. PRICE. With a Frontispiece by HAL LUDLOW. Crown 8vo, cloth extra, 3s. 6d.; post 8vo, illustrated boards, 2s.

Proctor (Richd. A.), Works by:

Flowers of the Sky. With 55 Illustrations. Small crown 8vo, cloth extra, 4s. 6d.

Easy Star Lessons. With Star Maps for Every Night in the Year, Drawings of the Constellations, &c. Crown 8vo, cloth extra, 6s.

Familiar Science Studies. Crown 8vo, cloth extra, 7s. 6d.

Myths and Marvels of Astronomy. Crown 8vo, cloth extra, 6s.

Pleasant Ways in Science. Crown 8vo, cloth extra, 6s.

Rough Ways made Smooth: A Series of Familiar Essays on Scientific Subjects. Crown 8vo, cloth extra, 6s.

R. A. Proctor's Works, *continued—*

Our Place among Infinities: A Series of Essays contrasting our Little Abode in Space and Time with the Infinities Around us. Crown 8vo, cloth extra, **6s.**

The Expanse of Heaven: A Series of Essays on the Wonders of the Firmament. Cr. 8vo, cloth extra, **6s.**

Saturn and its System. New and Revised Edition, with 13 Steel Plates. Demy 8vo, cloth extra, **10s. 6d.**

The Great Pyramid: Observatory, Tomb, and Temple. With Illustrations. Crown 8vo, cloth extra, **6s.**

Mysteries of Time and Space. With Illustrations. Crown 8vo, cloth extra, **7s. 6d.**

Wages and Wants of Science Workers. Crown 8vo, **1s. 6d.**

Pyrotechnist's Treasury (The): or, Complete Art of Making Fireworks. By THOMAS KENTISH. With numerous Illustrations. Crown 8vo, cloth extra, **4s. 6d.**

Rabelais' Works. Faithfully Translated from the French, with variorum Notes, and numerous characteristic Illustrations by GUSTAVE DORÉ. Crown 8vo, cloth extra, **7s. 6d.**

Rambosson.—Popular Astronomy. By J. RAMBOSSON, Laureate of the Institute of France. Translated by C. B. PITMAN. Crown 8vo, cloth gilt, with numerous Illustrations, and a beautifully executed Chart of Spectra, **7s. 6d.**

Reader's Handbook (The) of Allusions, References, Plots, and Stories. By the Rev. Dr. BREWER. Third Edition, revised throughout, with a New Appendix, containing a COMPLETE ENGLISH BIBLIOGRAPHY. Crown 8vo, 1,400 pages, cloth extra, **7s. 6d.**

Reade (Charles, D.C.L.), Novels by. Each post 8vo, illustrated boards, **2s.**; or crown 8vo, cloth extra, Illustrated, **3s. 6d.**

Peg Woffington. Illustrated by S. L. FILDES, A.R.A.

Christie Johnstone. Illustrated by WILLIAM SMALL.

It is Never Too Late to Mend. Illustrated by G. J. PINWELL.

The Course of True Love Never did run Smooth. Illustrated by HELEN PATERSON.

Charles Reade's Novels, *continued—*

The Autobiography of a Thief; Jack of all Trades; and James Lambert. Illustrated by MATT STRETCH.

Love me Little, Love me Long. Illustrated by M. ELLEN EDWARDS.

The Double Marriage. Illustrated by Sir JOHN GILBERT, R.A., and CHARLES KEENE.

The Cloister and the Hearth. Illustrated by CHARLES KEENE.

Hard Cash. Illustrated by F. W. LAWSON.

Griffith Gaunt. Illustrated by S. L. FILDES, A.R.A., and WM. SMALL.

Foul Play. Illustrated by GEORGE DU MAURIER.

Put Yourself in His Place. Illustrated by ROBERT BARNES.

A Terrible Temptation. Illustrated by EDWARD HUGHES and A. W. COOPER.

The Wandering Heir. Illustrated by HELEN PATERSON, S. L. FILDES, A.R.A., CHARLES GREEN, and HENRY WOODS, A.R.A.

A Simpleton. Illustrated by KATE CRAUFORD.

A Woman-Hater. Illustrated by THOS. COULDERY.

Readiana. With a Steel Plate Portrait of CHARLES READE.

A New Collection of Stories. In Three Vols., crown 8vo. [*Preparing.*

Richardson. — A Ministry of Health, and other Papers. By BENJAMIN WARD RICHARDSON, M.D., &c. Crown 8vo, cloth extra, **6s.**

Riddell (Mrs. J. H.), Novels by:

Her Mother's Darling. Crown 8vo, cloth extra, **3s. 6d.**; post 8vo, illustrated boards, **2s.**

The Prince of Wales's Garden Party, and other Stories. With a Frontispiece by M. ELLEN EDWARDS. Crown 8vo, cloth extra, **3s. 6d.**

Rimmer (Alfred), Works by:

Our Old Country Towns. By ALFRED RIMMER. With over 50 Illustrations by the Author. Square 8vo, cloth extra, gilt, **10s. 6d.**

Rambles Round Eton and Harrow. By ALFRED RIMMER. With 50 Illustrations by the Author. Square 8vo, cloth gilt, **10s. 6d.**

About England with Dickens. With 58 Illustrations by ALFRED RIMMER and C. A. VANDERHOOF. Square 8vo, cloth gilt, **10s. 6d.**

Robinson (F. W.), Novels by:

Women are Strange, &c. Three Vols., crown 8vo, 31s. 6d

The Hands of Justice. Three Vols., crown 8vo, 31s. 6d.

Robinson.—The Poets Birds. By PHIL. ROBINSON, Author of "Noah's Ark," &c. Cr. 8vo, cloth extra, 7s. 6d.

Robinson Crusoe : A beautiful reproduction of Major's Edition, with 37 Woodcuts and Two Steel Plates by GEORGE CRUIKSHANK, choicely printed. Crown 8vo, cloth extra, 7s. 6d. A few Large-Paper copies, printed on hand-made paper, with India proofs of the Illustrations, price 36s. [*In preparation.*]

Rochefoucauld's Maxims and Moral Reflections. With Notes, and an Introductory Essay by SAINTE-BEUVE. Post 8vo, cloth limp, 2s.

Roll of Battle Abbey, The ; or. A List of the Principal Warriors who came over from Normandy with William the Conqueror, and Settled in this Country, A.D. 1066-7. With the principal Arms emblazoned in Gold and Colours. Handsomely printed, price 5s.

Ross.—Behind a Brass Knocker: Some Grim Realities in Picture and Prose. By FRED. BARNARD and C. H. ROSS. Demy 8vo, cloth extra, with 30 full-page Drawings, 10s. 6d.

Rowley (Hon. Hugh), Works by:

Post 8vo, cloth limp, 2s. 6d. each.

Puniana: Riddles and Jokes. With numerous Illustrations.

More Puniana. Profusely Illustrated.

Sala.—Gaslight and Daylight. By GEORGE AUGUSTUS SALA. Post 8vo, illustrated boards. 2s.

Sanson.—Seven Generations of Executioners: Memoirs of the Sanson Family (1688 to 1847). Edited by HENRY SANSON. Crown 8vo, cloth extra, 3s. 6d.

Saunders (John), Novels by:

Crown 8vo, cloth extra, 3s. 6d. each ; or post 8vo, illustrated boards, 2s. each.

Bound to the Wheel.

One Against the World.

Guy Waterman.

The Lion in the Path.

The Two Dreamers.

Scott (Sir Walter).—The Lady of the Lake. With 120 fine Illustrations. Small 4to, pine-wood binding, 16s.

"Secret Out" Series, The :

Crown 8vo, cloth extra, profusely Illustrated, 4s. 6d. each.

The Secret Out: One Thousand Tricks with Cards, and other Recreations; with Entertaining Experiments in Drawing-room or "White Magic." By W. H. CREMER. 300 Engravings.

The Pyrotechnist's Treasury; or, Complete Art of Making Fireworks. By THOMAS KENTISH. With numerous Illustrations.

The Art of Amusing: A Collection of Graceful Arts, Games, Tricks, Puzzles, and Charades. By FRANK BELLEW. With 300 Illustrations.

Hanky Panky : Very Easy Tricks, Very Difficult Tricks, White Magic, Sleight of Hand. Edited by W. H. CREMER. With 200 Illustrations.

The Merry Circle: A Book of New Intellectual Games and Amusements. By CLARA BELLEW. Many Illusts.

Magician's Own Book: Performances with Cups and Balls, Eggs, Hats, Handkerchiefs, &c. All from actual Experience. Edited by W. H. CREMER. 200 Illustrations.

Magic No Mystery : Tricks with Cards, Dice, Balls, &c., with fully descriptive Directions; the Art of Secret Writing ; Training of Performing Animals, &c. Coloured Frontispiece and many Illustrations.

Senior (William), Works by :

Travel and Trout in the Antipodes. Crown 8vo, cloth extra, 6s.

By Stream and Sea. Post 8vo, cloth limp, 2s. 6d.

Shakespeare :

The First Folio Shakespeare.—MR. WILLIAM SHAKESPEARE'S Comedies, Histories, and Tragedies. Published according to the true Originall Copies. London, Printed by ISAAC IAGGARD and ED. BLOUNT. 1623.—A Reproduction of the extremely rare original, in reduced facsimile, by a photographic process—ensuring the strictest accuracy in every detail. Small 8vo, half-Roxburghe, 7s. 6d.

The Lansdowne Shakespeare. Beautifully printed in red and black, in small but very clear type. With engraved facsimile of DROESHOUT's Portrait. Post 8vo, cloth extra, 7s. 6d.

SHAKESPEARE, *continued*—

Shakespeare for Children: Tales from Shakespeare. By CHARLES and MARY LAMB. With numerous Illustrations, coloured and plain, by J. MOYR SMITH. Crown 4to, cloth gilt, 6s.

The **Handbook of Shakespeare Music**. Being an Account of 350 Pieces of Music, set to Words taken from the Plays and Poems of Shakespeare, the compositions ranging from the Elizabethan Age to the Present Time. By ALFRED ROFFE. 4to, half-Roxburghe, 7s.

A **Study of Shakespeare**. By ALGERNON CHARLES SWINBURNE. Crown 8vo, cloth extra, 8s.

Shelley's Complete Works, in Four Vols., post 8vo, cloth limp, 8s.; or separately, 2s. each. Vol. I. contains his Early Poems, Queen Mab, &c., with an Introduction by LEIGH HUNT; Vol. II., his Later Poems, Laon and Cythna, &c.; Vol. III., Posthumous Poems, the Shelley Papers, &c.; Vol. IV., his Prose Works, including A Refutation of Deism, Zastrozzi, St. Irvyne, &c.

Sheridan's Complete Works, with Life and Anecdotes. Including his Dramatic Writings, printed from the Original Editions, his Works in Prose and Poetry, Translations, Speeches, Jokes, Puns, &c. With a Collection of Sheridaniana. Crown 8vo, cloth extra, gilt, with 10 full-page Tinted Illustrations, 7s. 6d.

Short Sayings of Great Men. With Historical and Explanatory Notes by SAMUEL A. BENT, M.A. Demy 8vo, cloth extra, 7s. 6d.

Sidney's (Sir Philip) Complete Poetical Works, including all those in "Arcadia." With Portrait, Memorial-Introduction, Essay on the Poetry of Sidney, and Notes, by the Rev. A. B. GROSART, D.D. Three Vols., crown 8vo, cloth boards, 18s.

Signboards: Their History. With Anecdotes of Famous Taverns and Remarkable Characters. By JACOB LARWOOD and JOHN CAMDEN HOTTEN. Crown 8vo, cloth extra, with 100 Illustrations, 7s. 6d.

Sketchley.—A Match in the Dark. By ARTHUR SKETCHLEY. Post 8vo, illustrated boards, 2s.

Slang Dictionary, The: Etymological, Historical, and Anecdotal. Crown 8vo, cloth extra, gilt, 6s. 6d.

Smith (J. Moyr), Works by :

The **Prince of Argolis**: A Story of the Old Greek Fairy Time. By J. MOYR SMITH. Small 8vo, cloth extra, with 130 Illustrations, 3s. 6d.

Tales of Old Thule. Collected and Illustrated by J. MOYR SMITH. Crown 8vo, cloth gilt, profusely Illustrated, 6s.

The **Wooing of the Water Witch**: A Northern Oddity. By EVAN DALDORNE. Illustrated by J. MOYR SMITH. Small 8vo, cloth extra, 6s.

South-West, The New: Travelling Sketches from Kansas, New Mexico, Arizona, and Northern Mexico. By ERNST VON HESSE-WARTEGG. With 100 fine Illustrations and 3 Maps. 8vo, cloth extra, 14s.   [*In preparation.*

Spalding.—Elizabethan Demonology: An Essay in Illustration of the Belief in the Existence of Devils, and the Powers possessed by Them. By T. ALFRED SPALDING, LL.B. Crown 8vo, cloth extra, 5s.

Speight. — The Mysteries of Heron Dyke. By T. W. SPEIGHT. With a Frontispiece by M. ELLEN EDWARDS. Crown 8vo, cloth extra, 3s. 6d.; post 8vo, illustrated boards, 2s.

Spenser for Children. By M. H. TOWRY. With Illustrations by WALTER J. MORGAN. Crown 4to, with Coloured Illustrations, cloth gilt, 6s.

Staunton.—Laws and Practice of Chess; Together with an Analysis of the Openings, and a Treatise on End Games. By HOWARD STAUNTON. Edited by ROBERT B. WORMALD. A New Edition, small crown 8vo, cloth extra, 5s.

Stedman. — Victorian Poets: Critical Essays. By EDMUND CLARENCE STEDMAN. Crown 8vo, cloth extra, 9s

Sterndale.—The Afghan Knife: A Novel. By ROBERT ARMITAGE STERNDALE, F.R.G.S. Crown 8vo, cloth extra, 3s. 6d.; post 8vo, illustrated boards, 2s.   [*Shortly.*

Stevenson (R. Louis), Works by:
Familiar Studies of Men and Books. Crown 8vo, cloth extra, 6s.
New Arabian Nights. New and Cheaper Edition. Crown 8vo, cloth extra, 6s.

St. John.—A Levantine Family. By BAYLE ST. JOHN. Post 8vo, illustrated boards, 2s.

Stoddard.—Summer Cruising in the South Seas. By CHARLES WARREN STODDARD. Illustrated by WALLIS MACKAY. Crown 8vo, cloth extra, 3s. 6d.

St. Pierre.—Paul and Virginia, and The Indian Cottage. By BERNARDIN DE ST. PIERRE. Edited, with Life, by the Rev. E. CLARKE. Post 8vo, cloth limp, 2s.

Strahan.—Twenty Years of a Publisher's Life. By ALEXANDER STRAHAN. Two Vols., crown 8vo, with numerous Portraits and Illustrations, 24s. [In preparation.

Strutt's Sports and Pastimes of the People of England; including the Rural and Domestic Recreations, May Games, Mummeries, Shows, Processions, Pageants, and Pompous Spectacles, from the Earliest Period to the Present Time. With 140 Illustrations. Edited by WILLIAM HONE. Crown 8vo, cloth extra, 7s. 6d.

Suburban Homes (The) of London: A Residential Guide to Favourite London Localities, their Society, Celebrities, and Associations. With Notes on their Rental, Rates, and House Accommodation. With a Map of Suburban London. Crown 8vo, cloth extra, 7s. 6d.

Swift's Choice Works, in Prose and Verse. With Memoir, Portrait, and Facsimiles of the Maps in the Original Edition of "Gulliver's Travels." Cr. 8vo, cloth extra, 7s. 6d.

Swinburne (Algernon C.), Works by:
The Queen Mother and Rosamond. Fcap. 8vo, 5s.
Atalanta in Calydon. Crown 8vo, 6s.
Chastelard. A Tragedy. Crown 8vo, 7s.

SWINBURNE'S WORKS, *continued*—
Poems and Ballads. FIRST SERIES. Fcap. 8vo, 9s. Also in crown 8vo, at same price.
Poems and Ballads. SECOND SERIES. Fcap. 8vo, 9s. Also in crown 8vo, at same price.
Notes on Poems and Reviews. 8vo, 1s.
William Blake: A Critical Essay. With Facsimile Paintings. Demy 8vo, 16s.
Songs before Sunrise. Crown 8vo, 10s. 6d.
Bothwell: A Tragedy. Crown 8vo, 12s. 6d.
George Chapman: An Essay. Crown 8vo, 7s.
Songs of Two Nations. Crown 8vo, 6s.
Essays and Studies. Crown 8vo, 12s.
Erechtheus: A Tragedy. Crown 8vo, 6s.
Note of an English Republican on the Muscovite Crusade. 8vo, 1s.
A Note on Charlotte Bronte. Crown 8vo, 6s.
A Study of Shakespeare. Crown 8vo, 8s.
Songs of the Springtides. Crown 8vo, 6s.
Studies in Song. Crown 8vo, 7s.
Mary Stuart: A Tragedy. Crown 8vo, 9s.
Tristram of Lyonesse, and other Poems. Crown 8vo, 9s.
A Century of Roundels. Small 4to, cloth extra, 8s. [In preparation.

Syntax's (Dr.) Three Tours: In Search of the Picturesque, in Search of Consolation, and in Search of a Wife. With the whole of Rowlandson's droll page Illustrations in Colours and a Life of the Author by J. C. HOTTEN. Medium 8vo, cloth extra, 7s. 6d.

Taine's History of English Literature. Translated by HENRY VAN LAUN. Four Vols., small 8vo, cloth boards, 30s.—POPULAR EDITION, in Two Vols., crown 8vo, cloth extra, 15s.

Taylor's (Bayard) Diversions of the Echo Club: Burlesques of Modern Writers. Post 8vo, cloth limp, 2s.

Taylor's (Tom) Historical Dramas: "Clancarty," "Jeanne Darc," "'Twixt Axe and Crown," "The Fool's Revenge," "Arkwright's Wife," "Anne Boleyn," "Plot and Passion." One Vol., crown 8vo, cloth extra, 7s. 6d.

. The Plays may also be had separately, at 1s. each.

Thackerayana: Notes and Anecdotes. Illustrated by Hundreds of Sketches by WILLIAM MAKEPEACE THACKERAY, depicting Humorous Incidents in his School-life, and Favourite Characters in the books of his every-day reading. With Coloured Frontispiece. Crown 8vo, cloth extra, 7s. 6d.

Thomas (Bertha), Novels by:
Each crown 8vo, cloth extra, 3s. 6d.; or post 8vo, illustrated boards, 2s.

   Cressida.

   Proud Maisie.

   The Violin-Player.

Thomson's Seasons and Castle of Indolence. With a Biographical and Critical Introduction by ALLAN CUNNINGHAM, and over 50 fine Illustrations on Steel and Wood. Crown 8vo, cloth extra, gilt edges, 7s. 6d.

Thornbury (Walter), Works by:
Haunted London. Edited by EDWARD WALFORD, M.A. With Illustrations by F. W. FAIRHOLT, F.S.A. Crown 8vo, cloth extra, 7s. 6d.

The Life and Correspondence of J. M. W. Turner. Founded upon Letters and Papers furnished by his Friends and fellow Academicians. With numerous Illustrations in Colours, facsimiled from Turner's Original Drawings. Crown 8vo, cloth extra, 7s. 6d.

Old Stories Re-told. Post 8vo, cloth limp, 2s. 6d.

Tales for the Marines. Post 8vo, illustrated boards, 2s.

Timbs (John), Works by:
The History of Clubs and Club Life in London. With Anecdotes of its Famous Coffee-houses, Hostelries, and Taverns. With numerous Illustrations. Crown 8vo, cloth extra, 7s. 6d.

TIMBS' WORKS, *continued—*
English Eccentrics and Eccentricities: Stories of Wealth and Fashion, Delusions, Impostures, and Fanatic Missions, Strange Sights and Sporting Scenes, Eccentric Artists, Theatrical Folks, Men of Letters, &c. With nearly 50 Illusts. Crown 8vo, cloth extra, 7s. 6d.

Torrens. — The Marquess Wellesley, Architect of Empire. An Historic Portrait. By W. M. TORRENS, M.P. Demy 8vo, cloth extra, 14s.

Trollope (Anthony), Novels by:
The Way We Live Now. With Illustrations. Crown 8vo, cloth extra, 3s. 6d.; post 8vo, illust. boards, 2s.

The American Senator. Crown 8vo, cloth extra, 3s. 6d.; post 8vo, illustrated boards, 2s.

Kept in the Dark. With a Frontispiece by J. E. MILLAIS, R.A. Two Vols., post 8vo, 12s.

Frau Frohmann, &c. With Frontispiece. Crown 8vo, cloth extra, 3s. 6d.

Marion Fay. Cr. 8vo, cl. extra, 3s. 6d.

Mr. Scarborough's Family. Three Vols., crown 8vo, 31s. 6d.

Trollope (T. A.).—Diamond Cut Diamond, and other Stories. By THOMAS ADOLPHUS TROLLOPE. Crown 8vo, cloth extra, 3s. 6d.; post 8vo, illustrated boards, 2s.

Turner's Rivers of England: Sixteen Drawings by J. M. W. TURNER, R.A., and Three by THOMAS GIRTIN. Mezzotinted by THOMAS LUPTON, CHARLES TURNER, and other Engravers. With Descriptions by Mrs. HOFLAND. A New Edition, reproduced by Heliograph. Edited by W. COSMO MONKHOUSE, Author of "The Life of Turner" in the "Great Artists" Series. Large folio, 31s. 6d.   [*Shortly.*

Tytler (Sarah), Novels by:
What She Came Through. Crown 8vo, cloth extra, 3s. 6d.; post 8vo, illustrated boards, 2s.

The Bride's Pass. With a Frontispiece by P. MACNAB. Crown 8vo, cloth extra, 3s. 6d.

Van Laun.—History of French Literature. By HENRI VAN LAUN. Complete in Three Vols., demy 8vo, cloth boards, 22s. 6d.

Villari. — A Double Bond: A Story. By LINDA VILLARI. Fcap. 8vo, picture cover, 1s.

Walcott.—Church Work and Life in English Minsters; and the English Student's Monasticon. By the Rev. MACKENZIE E. C. WALCOTT, B.D. Two Vols., crown 8vo, cloth extra, with Map and Ground-Plans, 14s.

Walford.—The County Families of the United Kingdom. By ED-WARD WALFORD, M.A. Containing Notices of the Descent, Birth, Marriage, Education, &c., of more than 12,000 distinguished Heads of Families, their Heirs Apparent or Presumptive, the Offices they hold or have held, their Town and Country Addresses, Clubs, &c. The Twenty-third Annual Edition, for 1883, cloth, full gilt, 50s.

Walton and Cotton's Complete Angler; or, The Contemplative Man's Recreation; being a Discourse of Rivers, Fishponds, Fish and Fishing, written by IZAAK WALTON; and Instructions how to Angle for a Trout or Grayling in a clear Stream, by CHARLES COTTON. With Original Memoirs and Notes by Sir HARRIS NICOLAS, and 61 Copperplate Illustrations. Large crown 8vo, cloth antique, 7s. 6d.

Wanderer's Library, The:

Crown 8vo, cloth extra, 3s. 6d. each.

Wanderings in Patagonia; or, Life among the Ostrich Hunters. By JULIUS BEERBOHM. Illustrated.

Camp Notes: Stories of Sport and Adventure in Asia, Africa, and America. By FREDERICK BOYLE.

Savage Life. By FREDERICK BOYLE.

Merrie England in the Olden Time. By GEORGE DANIEL. With Illustrations by ROBT. CRUIKSHANK.

Circus Life and Circus Celebrities. By THOMAS FROST.

The Lives of the Conjurers. By THOMAS FROST.

The Old Showmen and the Old London Fairs. By THOMAS FROST.

Low Life Deeps. An Account of the Strange Fish to be found there. By JAMES GREENWOOD

The Wilds of London. By JAMES GREENWOOD.

Tunis: The Land and the People. By the Chevalier de HESSE-WAR-TEGG. With 22 Illustrations.

The Life and Adventures of a Cheap Jack. By One of the Fraternity. Edited by CHARLES HINDLEY.

WANDERER'S LIBRARY, *continued—*

The World Behind the Scenes. By PERCY FITZGERALD.

Tavern Anecdotes and Sayings: Including the Origin of Signs, and Reminiscences connected with Taverns, Coffee Houses, Clubs, &c. By CHARLES HINDLEY. With Illustrations.

The Genial Showman: Life and Adventures of Artemus Ward. By E. P. HINGSTON. With a Frontispiece.

The Story of the London Parks. By JACOB LARWOOD. With Illusts.

London Characters. By HENRY MAYHEW. Illustrated.

Seven Generations of Executioners: Memoirs of the Sanson Family (1688 to 1847). Edited by HENRY SANSON.

Summer Cruising in the South Seas. By CHARLES WARREN STODDARD. Illust. by WALLIS MACKAY.

Warrants, &c. :—

Warrant to Execute Charles I. An exact Facsimile, with the Fifty nine Signatures, and corresponding Seals. Carefully printed on paper to imitate the Original, 22 in. by 14 in. Price 2s.

Warrant to Execute Mary Queen of Scots. An exact Facsimile, including the Signature of Queen Elizabeth, and a Facsimile of the Great Seal. Beautifully printed on paper to imitate the Original MS. Price 2s.

Magna Charta. An Exact Facsimile of the Original Document in the British Museum, printed on fine plate paper, nearly 3 feet long by 2 feet wide, with the Arms and Seals emblazoned in Gold and Colours. Price 5s.

The Roll of Battle Abbey; or, A List of the Principal Warriors who came over from Normandy with William the Conqueror, and Settled in this Country, A.D. 1066-7. With the principal Arms emblazoned in Gold and Colours. Price 5s.

Westropp.—Handbook of Pottery and Porcelain; or, History of those Arts from the Earliest Period. By HODDER M. WESTROPP. With numerous Illustrations, and a List of Marks. Crown 8vo, cloth limp, 4s. 6d.

Whistler v. Ruskin: Art and Art Critics. By J. A. MACNEILL WHISTLER. Seventh Edition, square 8vo, 1s.

White's Natural History of Selborne. Edited, with Additions, by THOMAS BROWN, F.L.S. Post 8vo, cloth limp, 2s.

Williams (W. Mattieu, F.R.A.S.), Works by:

Science in Short Chapters. Crown 8vo, cloth extra, 7s. 6d.

A Simple Treatise on Heat. Crown 8vo, cloth limp, with Illustrations, 2s. 6d.

Wilson (C.E.).—Persian Wit and Humour: Being the Sixth Book of the Baharistan of Jami, Translated for the first time from the Original Persian into English Prose and Verse. With Notes by C. E. WILSON, M.R.A.S., Assistant Librarian Royal Academy of Arts. Crown 8vo, parchment binding, 4s.

Wilson (Dr. Andrew, F.R.S.E.), Works by:

Chapters on Evolution: A Popular History of the Darwinian and Allied Theories of Development. Second Edition. Crown 8vo, cloth extra, with 259 Illustrations, 7s. 6d.

Leaves from a Naturalist's Notebook. Post 8vo, cloth limp, 2s. 6d.

Leisure-Time Studies, chiefly Biological. Second Edition. Crown 8vo, cloth extra, with Illustrations, 6s.

Winter (J. S.), Stories by:

Cavalry Life. Crown 8vo, cloth extra, 3s. 6d.

Regimental Legends. Three Vols., crown 8vo, 31s. 6d.

Wood.—Sabina: A Novel. By Lady WOOD. Post 8vo, illustrated boards, 2s.

Words, Facts, and Phrases: A Dictionary of Curious, Quaint, and Out-of-the-Way Matters. By ELIEZER EDWARDS. Crown 8vo, half-bound, 12s. 6d.

Wright (Thomas), Works by:

Caricature History of the Georges. (The House of Hanover.) With 400 Pictures, Caricatures, Squibs, Broadsides, Window Pictures, &c. Crown 8vo, cloth extra, 7s. 6d.

History of Caricature and of the Grotesque in Art, Literature, Sculpture, and Painting. Profusely Illustrated by F. W. FAIRHOLT, F.S.A. Large post 8vo, cloth extra, 7s. 6d.

Yates (Edmund), Novels by:

Post 8vo, illustrated boards, 2s. each.
Castaway.
The Forlorn Hope.
Land at Last.

NOVELS.

NEW NOVELS at every Library

Behind a Brass Knocker: Some Grim Realities in Picture and Prose. By FRED BARNARD and C. H. ROSS. Demy 8vo, cloth extra, with 30 full-page Drawings, 10s. 6d.

The Captains' Room, &c. By WALT. BESANT, Author of "All Sorts and Conditions of Men," &c. Three Vols.

Annan Water. By ROBERT BUCHANAN. Three Vols. [Shortly.

Heart and Science: A Story of the Present Day. By WILKIE COLLINS. Three Vols.

Port Salvation; or, The Evangelist. By ALPHONSE DAUDET. Translated by C. HARRY MELTZER. Two Vols., post 8vo, 12s.

Circe's Lovers. By J. LEITH DERWENT. Three Vols., cr. 8vo. [Shortly.

Of High Degree. By CHARLES GIBBON, Author of "Robin Gray," "The Golden Shaft," &c. Three Vols.

The Golden Shaft. By CHARLES GIBBON. Three Vols.

Fancy Free. By CHARLES GIBBON. Two Vols., crown 8vo. [Shortly.

Dust: A Story. By JULIAN HAWTHORNE, Author of "Garth," "Sebastian Strome," &c. Three Vols.

Self-Condemned. By Mrs. ALFRED HUNT. Three Vols.

Gideon Fleyce. By HENRY W. LUCY. Three Vols.

Val Strange. By D. CHRISTIE MURRAY. Three Vols.

Hearts. By DAVID CHRISTIE MURRAY. Three Vols.

By the Gate of the Sea. By DAVID CHRISTIE MURRAY. Two Vols., post 8vo, 12s. [Shortly.

Wanda. By OUIDA. Three Vols., crown 8vo.

Kit: A Memory. By JAMES PAYN. Three Vols.

A New Collection of Stories by CHARLES READE is now in preparation, in Three Vols.

The Hands of Justice. By F. W. ROBINSON. Three Vols.

Women are Strange, &c. By F. W. ROBINSON. Three Vols.

Kept in the Dark. By ANTHONY TROLLOPE. Two Vols. 12s.

Mr. Scarborough's Family. By ANTHONY TROLLOPE. Three Vols.

Regimental Legends. By J. S. WINTER. Three Vols.

THE PICCADILLY NOVELS:

Popular Stories by the Best Authors. LIBRARY EDITIONS, many Illustrated, crown 8vo, cloth extra, 3s. 6d. each.

BY MRS. ALEXANDER.
Maid, Wife, or Widow?

BY W. BESANT & JAMES RICE.
Ready-Money Mortiboy.
My Little Girl.
The Case of Mr. Lucraft.
This Son of Vulcan.
With Harp and Crown.
The Golden Butterfly.
By Celia's Arbour.
The Monks of Thelema.
'Twas in Trafalgar's Bay.
The Seamy Side.
The Ten Years' Tenant.
The Chaplain of the Fleet.

BY WALTER BESANT.
All Sorts and Conditions of Men.

BY ROBERT BUCHANAN.
A Child of Nature.
God and the Man.
The Shadow of the Sword.
The Martyrdom of Madeline.
Love Me for Ever.

BY MRS. H. LOVETT CAMERON.
Deceivers Ever. | Juliet's Guardian.

BY MORTIMER COLLINS.
Sweet Anne Page.
Transmigration.
From Midnight to Midnight.

MORTIMER & FRANCES COLLINS.
Blacksmith and Scholar.
The Village Comedy.
You Play me False.

BY WILKIE COLLINS.

Antonina.	Miss or Mrs?
Basil.	New Magdalen.
Hide and Seek.	The Frozen Deep.
The Dead Secret.	The Law and the
Queen of Hearts.	Lady.
My Miscellanies.	The Two Destinies
Woman in White.	Haunted Hotel.
The Moonstone.	The Fallen Leaves
Man and Wife.	Jezebel's Daughter
Poor Miss Finch.	The Black Robe.

Piccadilly Novels, *continued*

BY DUTTON COOK.
Paul Foster's Daughter.

BY WILLIAM CYPLES.
Hearts of Gold.

BY J. LEITH DERWENT
Our Lady of Tears.

BY M. BETHAM-EDWARDS.
Felicia.

BY MRS. ANNIE EDWARDES.
Archie Lovell.

BY R. E. FRANCILLON.
Olympia.
Queen Cophetua.
One by One.

BY EDWARD GARRETT.
The Capel Girls.

BY CHARLES GIBBON.
Robin Gray.
For Lack of Gold.
In Love and War.
What will the World Say?
For the King.
In Honour Bound.
Queen of the Meadow.
In Pastures Green.
The Flower of the Forest.
A Heart's Problem.
The Braes of Yarrow.

BY THOMAS HARDY.
Under the Greenwood Tree.

BY JULIAN HAWTHORNE.
Garth.
Ellice Quentin.
Sebastian Strome.
Prince Saroni's Wife.

BY SIR A. HELPS.
Ivan de Biron.

BY MRS. ALFRED HUNT.
Thornicroft's Model.
The Leaden Casket.

BY JEAN INGELOW.
Fated to be Free.

BY HENRY JAMES, Jun.
Confidence.

BY HARRIETT JAY.
The Queen of Connaught.
The Dark Colleen.

Piccadilly Novels, *continued* —

BY HENRY KINGSLEY.
Number Seventeen.
Oakshott Castle.

BY E. LYNN LINTON.
Patricia Kemball.
Atonement of Leam Dundas
The World Well Lost.
Under which Lord?
With a Silken Thread.
The Rebel of the Family.
"My Love!"

BY JUSTIN McCARTHY, M.P.
The Waterdale Neighbours.
My Enemy's Daughter.
Linley Rochford.
A Fair Saxon.
Dear Lady Disdain.
Miss Misanthrope.
Donna Quixote.
The Comet of a Season.

BY GEORGE MACDONALD, LL.D
Paul Faber, Surgeon.
Thomas Wingfold, Curate.

BY KATHARINE S. MACQUOID.
Lost Rose
The Evil Eye.

BY FLORENCE MARRYAT.
Open! Sesame!
Written In Fire.

BY JEAN MIDDLEMASS.
Touch and Go.

BY D. CHRISTIE MURRAY.
A Life's Atonement.
Joseph's Coat.
Coals of Fire.
A Model Father.

BY MRS. OLIPHANT.
Whiteladies.

BY JAMES PAYN.

Lost Sir Massing- berd.	High Spirits. Under One Roof.
Best of Husbands	Carlyon's Year.
Fallen Fortunes.	A Confidential Agent.
Halves.	
Walter's Word.	From Exile.
What He Cost Her	A Grape from a Thorn.
Less Black than We're Painted.	For Cash Only
By Proxy.	

PICCADILLY NOVELS, *continued—*

BY E. C. PRICE.

Valentina.

BY CHARLES READE, D.C.L.

It Is Never Too Late to Mend.
Hard Cash.
Peg Woffington.
Christie Johnstone.
Griffith Gaunt.
The Double Marriage.
Love Me Little, Love Me Long.
Foul Play.
A Simpleton.
The Cloister and the Hearth.
The Course of True Love.
The Autobiography of a Thief.
Put Yourself in His Place.
A Terrible Temptation.
The Wandering Heir.
A Woman-Hater.
Readiana.

BY MRS. J. H. RIDDELL.

Her Mother's Darling.
Prince of Wales's Garden Party.

BY JOHN SAUNDERS.

Bound to the Wheel.
Guy Waterman.
One Against the World.
The Lion in the Path.
The Two Dreamers.

BY T. W. SPEIGHT.

The Mysteries of Heron Dyke.

BY R. A. STERNDALE.

The Afghan Knife.

BY BERTHA THOMAS.

Proud Maisie. | Cressida.
The Violin-Player.

BY ANTHONY TROLLOPE.

The Way we Live Now.
The American Senator.
Frau Frohmann.
Marion Fay.

BY T. A. TROLLOPE.

Diamond Cut Diamond.

BY SARAH TYTLER.

What She Came Through.
The Bride's Pass.

BY J. S. WINTER.

Cavalry Life.

Cheap Editions of POPULAR

NOVELS. Post 8vo, illustrated boards, 2s. each. [WILKIE COLLINS'S NOVELS and BESANT and RICE'S NOVELS may also be had in cloth limp at 2s. 6d. See, too, the PICCADILLY NOVELS, for Library Editions.]

BY EDMOND ABOUT.

The Fellah.

BY HAMILTON AÏDÉ.

Carr of Carrlyon.
Confidences.

BY MRS. ALEXANDER.

Maid, Wife, or Widow?

BY SHELSLEY BEAUCHAMP.

Grantley Grange.

BY W. BESANT & JAMES RICE.

Ready-Money Mortiboy.
With Harp and Crown.
This Son of Vulcan.
My Little Girl.
The Case of Mr. Lucraft.
The Golden Butterfly.
By Celia's Arbour.
The Monks of Thelema.
'Twas in Trafalgar's Bay.
The Seamy Side.
The Ten Years' Tenant.
The Chaplain of the Fleet.

BY FREDERICK BOYLE.

Camp Notes.
Savage Life.

BY BRET HARTE.

An Heiress of Red Dog.
Gabriel Conroy.
The Luck of Roaring Camp.
Flip.

BY ROBERT BUCHANAN.

The Shadow of the Sword.
A Child of Nature.

BY MRS. BURNETT.

Surly Tim.

BY MRS. LOVETT CAMERON.

Deceivers Ever.
Juliet's Guardian.

BY MACLAREN COBBAN.

The Cure of Souls.

BY C. ALLSTON COLLINS.

The Bar Sinister.

POPULAR NOVELS, *continued—*

BY WILKIE COLLINS.

Antonina.
Basil.
Hide and Seek.
The Dead Secret.
Queen of Hearts.
My Miscellanies.
The Woman in White.
The Moonstone.
Man and Wife.
Poor Miss Finch.
Miss or Mrs. ?
The New Magdalen.
The Frozen Deep.
The Law and the Lady.
The Two Destinies.
The Haunted Hotel.
The Fallen Leaves.
Jezebel's Daughter.
The Black Robe

BY MORTIMER COLLINS.

Sweet Anne Page.
Transmigration.
From Midnight to Midnight.
A Fight with Fortune.

BY MORTIMER AND FRANCES COLLINS.

Sweet and Twenty.
Frances.
Blacksmith and Scholar.
The Village Comedy.
You Play me False.

BY DUTTON COOK.

Leo.
Paul Foster's Daughter.

BY J. LEITH DERWENT.

Our Lady of Tears.

BY CHARLES DICKENS.

Sketches by Boz.
The Pickwick Papers.
Oliver Twist.
Nicholas Nickleby.

BY MRS. ANNIE EDWARDES.

A Point of Honour.
Archie Lovell.

BY M. BETHAM-EDWARDS.

Felicia.

POPULAR NOVELS, *continued—*

BY EDWARD EGGLESTON.

Roxy.

BY PERCY FITZGERALD.

Bella Donna.
Never Forgotten.
The Second Mrs. Tillotson.
Polly.
Seventy-five Brooke Street.

BY ALBANY DE FONBLANQUE.

Filthy Lucre.

BY R. E. FRANCILLON.

Olympia.
Queen Cophetua.
One by One.

BY EDWARD GARRETT.

The Capel Girls.

BY CHARLES GIBBON.

Robin Gray.
For Lack of Gold.
What will the World Say?
In Honour Bound.
The Dead Heart.
In Love and War.
For the King.
Queen of the Meadow.
In Pastures Green.

BY WILLIAM GILBERT.

Dr. Austin's Guests.
The Wizard of the Mountain.
James Duke.

BY JAMES GREENWOOD.

Dick Temple.

BY ANDREW HALLIDAY.

Every-Day Papers.

BY LADY DUFFUS HARDY.

Paul Wynter's Sacrifice.

BY THOMAS HARDY.

Under the Greenwood Tree.

BY JULIAN HAWTHORNE.

Garth.
Ellice Quentin.
Sebastian Strome.

BY SIR ARTHUR HELPS.

Ivan de Biron.

BY TOM HOOD.

A Golden Heart.

POPULAR NOVELS, *continued*—

BY VICTOR HUGO.

The Hunchback of Notre Dame.

BY MRS. ALFRED HUNT.

Thornicroft's Model.
The Leaden Casket.

BY JEAN INGELOW.

Fated to be Free.

BY HENRY JAMES, Jun.

Confidence.

BY HARRIETT JAY.

The Dark Colleen.
The Queen of Connaught.

BY HENRY KINGSLEY.

Oakshott Castle.
Number Seventeen.

BY E. LYNN LINTON.

Patricia Kemball.
The Atonement of Leam Dundas.
The World Well Lost.
Under which Lord?
With a Silken Thread.
The Rebel of the Family.
"My Love!"

BY JUSTIN McCARTHY, M.P.

Dear Lady Disdain.
The Waterdale Neighbours.
My Enemy's Daughter.
A Fair Saxon.
Linley Rochford.
Miss Misanthrope.
Donna Quixote.

BY GEORGE MACDONALD.

Paul Faber, Surgeon.
Thomas Wingfold, Curate.

BY MRS. MACDONELL.

Quaker Cousins.

BY KATHARINE S. MACQUOID.

The Evil Eye.
Lost Rose.

BY W. H. MALLOCK.

The New Republic.

BY FLORENCE MARRYAT.

Open! Sesame!
A Harvest of Wild Oats.
A Little Stepson.
Fighting the Air.
Written in Fire.

POPULAR NOVELS, *continued*—

BY JEAN MIDDLEMASS.

Touch and Go.
Mr. Dorillion.

BY D. CHRISTIE MURRAY.

A Life's Atonement.
A Model Father.

BY MRS. OLIPHANT.

Whiteladies.

BY MRS. ROBERT O'REILLY.

Phœbe's Fortunes.

BY OUIDA.

LIBRARY EDITIONS of OUIDA'S NOVELS may be had in crown 8vo, cloth extra, at 5s. each.

Held in Bondage.
Strathmore.
Chandos.
Under Two Flags.
Idalia.
Cecil Castlemaine.
Tricotrin.
Puck.
Folle Farine.
A Dog of Flanders.
Pascarel.
Two Little Wooden Shoes.
Signa.
In a Winter City.
Ariadne.
Friendship.
Moths.
Pipistrello.
A Village Commune.

BY JAMES PAYN.

Lost Sir Massingberd.
A Perfect Treasure.
Bentinck's Tutor.
Murphy's Master.
A County Family.
At Her Mercy.
A Woman's Vengeance.
Cecil's Tryst.
Clyffards of Clyffe
The Family Scapegrace.
Foster Brothers.
Found Dead.
Best of Husbands
Walter's Word.
Halves.
Fallen Fortunes.
What He Cost Her
Humorous Stories
Gwendoline's Harvest.
Like Father, Like Son.
A Marine Residence.
Married Beneath Him.
Mirk Abbey.
Not Wooed, but Won.
£200 Reward.
Less Black than We're Painted.
By Proxy.
Under One Roof.
High Spirits.
Carlyon's Year.
A Confidential Agent.
Some Private Views.
From Exile.

BY EDGAR A. POE.

The Mystery of Marie Roget.

POPULAR NOVELS, *continued*—

BY E. C. PRICE.
Valentina.

BY CHARLES READE.
It is Never Too Late to Mend.
Hard Cash.
Peg Woffington.
Christie Johnstone.
Griffith Gaunt.
Put Yourself in His Place.
The Double Marriage.
Love Me Little, Love Me Long.
Foul Play.
The Cloister and the Hearth.
The Course of True Love.
Autobiography of a Thief.
A Terrible Temptation.
The Wandering Heir.
A Simpleton.
A Woman-Hater.
Readiana.

BY MRS. RIDDELL.
Her Mother's Darling.

BY BAYLE ST. JOHN.
A Levantine Family.

BY GEORGE AUGUSTUS SALA.
Gaslight and Daylight.

BY JOHN SAUNDERS.
Bound to the Wheel.
One Against the World.
Guy Waterman.
The Lion in the Path.
The Two Dreamers.

BY ARTHUR SKETCHLEY.
A Match in the Dark.

BY T. W. SPEIGHT.
The Mysteries of Heron Dyke.

BY R. A. STERNDALE.
The Afghan Knife.

BY BERTHA THOMAS.
Cressida.
Proud Maisie.
The Violin-Player.

POPULAR NOVELS, *continued* —

BY WALTER THORNBURY.
Tales for the Marines.

BY T. ADOLPHUS TROLLOPE.
Diamond Cut Diamond.

BY ANTHONY TROLLOPE.
The Way We Live Now.
The American Senator.

BY MARK TWAIN.
Tom Sawyer.
An Idle Excursion.
A Pleasure Trip on the Continent
of Europe.

BY SARAH TYTLER.
What She Came Through.

BY LADY WOOD.
Sabina.

BY EDMUND YATES.
Castaway.
The Forlorn Hope.
Land at Last.

ANONYMOUS.
Paul Ferroll.
Why Paul Ferroll Killed his Wife.

Fcap. 8vo, picture covers, 1s. each.
Jeff Briggs's Love Story. By BRET HARTE.
The Twins of Table Mountain. By BRET HARTE.
Mrs. Gainsborough's Diamonds. By JULIAN HAWTHORNE.
Kathleen Mavourneen. By Author of "That Lass o' Lowrie's."
Lindsay's Luck. By the Author of "That Lass o' Lowrie's."
Pretty Polly Pemberton. By the Author of "That Lass o' Lowrie's."
Trooping with Crows. By Mrs. PIRKIS.
The Professor's Wife. By LEONARD GRAHAM.
A Double Bond. By LINDA VILLARI.
Esther's Glove. By R. E. FRANCILLON.
The Garden that Paid the Rent. By TOM JERROLD.

J. OGDEN AND CO., PRINTERS, 172, ST. JOHN STREET, E.C.